THE SCALP SLAYER

— by —

JONESY

AuthorHouse™ UK
1663 Liberty Drive
Bloomington, IN 47403 USA
www.authorhouse.co.uk
Phone: 0800.197.4150

Published by AuthorHouse 08/08/2016

ISBN: 978-1-5246-2981-6 (sc)
ISBN: 978-1-5246-2977-9 (hc)
ISBN: 978-1-5246-2978-6 (e)

CONTENTS

The most Horrifying story you ever read.
That will make the hairs stand up on your skin.

Chapter One

THE VICTIM

As Detective Jones stepped out of the vehicle. The rain brushed across his cheeks, while the wind was gently blowing. A flash of lightning lit the sky and he could see perched up against the wall a body, within the dark alleyway next to the Freeman Street Market. When detective Jones approached the body, he noticed that it was a young girl in her early twenties. With a big brown leather handbag, left beside the victim. Her golden curly long hair was missing from the top of her head, where the skin had been removed with the hair. There was blood running down the front of her head, that trickled down the both sides of the victim's nose. As the victim's body laid in an upright position. Her sharp brown eyes were wide open with the look of terror within them. The victim pink soft skin had turned a clammy colour, as cold as ice. Wearing a flowery dress that came to her knees, with a thin flowery belt that separated the top half of the dress from the bottom half. The legs had been split apart leaving a gap between them. A light coloured, tanned tights that had been frayed down one side. Red sandles on her feet. Detective Jones noticed the left sandal was half hanging off. He also noticed that the victim had blood seeping through her flowery dress around the stomach area.

The crime scene officer pulled up in their white van with the flashing blue light still going. She step out of the van and walks to the back. As the crime scene officer opened the back doors of the van and started to take equipment out. Before she decides to head into the crime scene area. The lights still went around on the van, as they lit up the alley. That was faded from the lighting as it lit the sky. The crime scene officer started to place lights around the alley and turned them on, causing the lights to blind the detective for a few seconds.

Detective Jones was a middle-age man wearing a long black coat that came down past his knees. Covering his black suit and white shirt with a multi-coloured tie that was neatly tied around his neck. His shoes were that shiny and black, you could see the lights reflecting off them clearly. His hair was light brown, that was covered by a black hat and his eyes were a green colour with a hint of brown in them. His pale white skin was starting to wrinkle, that made the detective Jones age more within the face.

"Detective Jones how are you?. I haven't seen you in a while. It must have been just over a month when I last saw you. Still think of you and that question you keep avoiding!, do you have the answer yet?".

The crime scene officer was a very slim woman with her jet black hair tied back into a ponytail. She had false contact lenses that covered her real colour eyes, by giving her eyes a bright red colour. With her light coloured skin and rosy red cheeks. Wearing a onesie white paper suit with a hood that covered her clothing and shoes. Also blue plastic gloves on both hands.

She was holding a big silver case in her left hand, leaving the other hand free for her to shake the detective's hand. While she was speaking to detective Jones. The case had number locks at the top just either side of the handle and black rubber trim that went around the edges of the case. Placing the case carefully on the floor next to the victim. So that the chemical substances used for bringing blood stains up, wouldn't get damaged and cross-contaminate any equipment that was contained in the case. The chemical substance was contained in a brown glass bottle that kept it at the right temperature, by giving the best results when using the chemical substance. She bent over to open the case with the number locks. Pulling out a mask which she had ready to placed over her mouth and nose. Putting eye goggles at the top of head ready to pull down, that rested between the top of the nose and on the hairline. She then started to prepare the area for examination, so that she was able to complete the examination on the victim as quickly and effectively. To make the area clear in time, for it to be open again before rush hour started.

"I know it has been a while. I've been working in London for six month's. I was under cover for the case, that I have been working on up here. Which was later found out that the people behind it run most of England's drug crime and where based in the London area. I was called in by Scotland Yard to take the job and was given a new identification. As I had the knowledge of the case and the people who ran the drug deals. They didn't know me as a detective at that time. So I gathered as much information on the case as I could, then handed it over to Scotland Yard. They decided that it will need the special forces to take over the case file. Sophia how are you and the kids doing?. I will have to pop around for a drink sometime so we can spend some time together. That question you asked, I will answer that question. But this is not the place or time ".

Looking straight into Sophia's eyes as he speaks to her.

"Ok on the answer to that question for now, that I have been waiting for. Which as been a while, to hear from you. Yes, you should come around sometime to spend time with me and the kids it would be nice and the kids have been missing you. They always ask where you are and I have to tell them you'll away on business. I know we are just friends with benefits at the moment, but you have to understand that the kids see you as a dad. They think we are a couple, which wouldn't be a bad thing would it now. All you have to do is give me the answer to the question when you are ready and you will never want to go back to the life you live now. Leave it at that, think about it. You're not getting any younger. Me and the kids are just fine".

lowering her tone to a soft voice that made the detective smile within his self, still putting on his fake straight face. Then turning and walking away to leave Sophia to do her job, which was hurtful to her. By giving her an empty feeling in her gut as detective Jones, showed no emotion in the face when walking away.

As Sophia knelt down next to the victim's body. She place's the face mask over her mouth and nose, pulling down the goggles over her eyes. Putting her hand into the pocket she pulled out a white chalk that was resting in the left pocket of her onesie. Sophia carefully drew around the victim body, leaving a print out of the body along the floor and so far up the wall. She then placed the chalk back into her pocket and carefully moved the victim onto the floor. So the victim was laid out straight, with her head resting on the pathway. As the victim's body went stiff it caused it to curve slightly when laid out on the floor. But Sophia didn't want to destroy any evidence that could be found when she examined the body back at the morgue. While she did the autopsy on the victim. So Sophia left the victim body the way it was. She knew the only way was by breaking the bones of the victim. This was the only way to actually straighten the body as rigamortis had already set in, causing the body to stiffen and prevent the bones from straightening. Sophia bent over the big case and grabbed her tweezers out. Carefully used the tweezers to route through the victim's body and then opened the large brown leather bag that was on the side of the victim. Taking out any evidence that could help with the investigation. Putting the evidence she had found into a plastic bag with a seal on it. by Sophia doing this it would keep the evidence from damage or cross-contamination and to prevent any damage to fingerprints that might be left by the murderer. As all the evidence went back to lock up at the police station. Would be tested for fingerprints and ran though the computer for matching fingerprints to the person it had been left by. As the evidence's slid into the plastic bags, Sophia sealed the bags up with the evidence in them. After doing this, Sophia wrote the date, time on all of the bags and placed each bag down. Where the evidence was found. By laying all the evidence that were bagged on the floor next to the victim body and placed triangle shape object that contained a letter on one side. Down beside each evidence that had been laid out around the victim's body. Including the victim, where Sophia placed the triangle down. just between the arm and body of the victim.

"Detective Jones".

Sophia called out with a loud tone, which echoes through the alleyway.

Detective Jones stubs his cigarette end out underneath his foot, twisting it a couple of times. Which left tobacco floating in a thin stream of water that the rain made, as it hit the surface of the pavement. Running in the direction of the roadside, then disappearing into the drains. As he walked toward Sophia who was still knelt down over the body. He pulled out his small black notebook from inside his long black coat. He jerks his wrist to flick the notebook open and with his other hand. Clicking the pen with the tip of the thumb ready to write down and take notes. For later when typing the statement out, so that the important evidence has been noted down for detective Jones to check back later.

"Yes, what do we have then?".

In his deep strong voice.

"Well as you can see the victim has a lock of hair with skin missing from the crown. The skull of the head can be seen where the skin and hair use to be. By looking at the skin that remains around the skull, you can see the zig zag around the edges of the skin as it became separated from the missing skin. That means the murderer used a jagged sharp object of some sort, to remove the skin and hair from the head. Which also appears to leave a number of marking on the skull, as the murderer carved into the skin with a jagged object. Causing the object to scrape the surface of the skull. That give's me an idea, the murderer sliced at a thirty degree's angle, carving it like a Sunday joint of meat. Which I will be able to confirm the correct angle and jagged object back at the morgue. Also showed from the marking that the murderer started from left to the right. If you take a look across the skull you can see teeth marking's digging into skull. The example here is a hole you are able to see in the skull. The teeth mark's showing on the skull are facing left, causing abrasions in the direction of the jagged points. While cutting left the teeth of the object used will pierce hole's as the object slices through the skin and scrape along the skull. Another example is causing the brain to shake as the murderer cut through. Which means that the murderer caused too many jerks when cutting into the skin. The brain fluid will drain from the right ear as it builds up pressure inside, causing the skin in the ear to pop".

Sophia leans over to lift the right side of the victim's hair and pointed with her index finger. Showing detective Jones, the fluid that was dripping out of the ear.

"There you go see the clear pinkish or reddish fluid dribbling out of the right ear. This shows the brain had been jerked to the right when cutting from the left. If you apply too much pressure when cutting on the left, this would cause the fluid to move inside the skull. That protect the brain, making the fluid go into the right ear. Causing the ear to fill up with fluid and creating a bubble effect underneath the skin, inside the ear. Like filling a water balloon up, till the balloon is unable to hold the water it burst out. The same effect will happen to the ear as the brain fluid builds up from underneath the skin inside the ear. Till the ear can't stretch anymore, causing the bubble to burst. Once that has occurred the fluid enters into the ear, dispersing out of the right ear. This determines that I have a general idea that the murderer is left handed.

At this moment, Sophia paused for a few second and gasped a breath, before speaking again. She looks down at the stomach area of the victim, where the blood had seeped through the flowery dress. Turning for a second while she takes out the surgical knife from the case. Sophia then carefully cutting the dress to leave a big enough gap to see where the blood was coming from, within the stomach area.

"If you look down here where the stomach area is. You will notice that the stomach has been sliced open by something. This is totally different from the jagged object, like the murderer has taken time and been very precise when slicing the stomach. Give and take I think the length of the cut is around five to six inches across the bottom of the stomach. There is something not right here, the skin of the stomach has been pulled apart, leaving the intestines exposed. You can tell as you look here at the start of the cut and then over here at the end of the cut. The skin as ripped slightly at both ends. This is caused by the skin being pulled apart and causing the skin to become weak and rip. I will be able to give you more detail's on that area when we get the victim to the morgue and open the victim's stomach to find out why the murderer has cut this area on the victim body".

At this point, Sophia stopped talking while she did a thorough check over the legs and feet of the victim. She lifted the foot that had the red sandal half hanging off. Sophia removed the sandle and placed the sandal on the floor, just beside her. Still holding the foot up, in her hand. She used her index finger to point at the next evidence found on the victim's body.

"Well by these abrasions you can just see through the tights, on the heels of her feet. These are caused by the victim being dragged. If you take a look at the sandal on the floor, you will notice the sandals have been scratched at the back of them. By the way, the left sandal was half hanging off the victim's foot. I believe the victim was not murdered in this area. Also from the amount of blood that's spilled on the floor around the victim and by the scratches on the sandals. It looks as if the victim body has been moved. The victim has been dead for more than twelve hours as the rigamortis has set in and the temperature of the body has dropped. Which means the murderer dragged the victim and left the victim body here to be found. The murderer could have been disturbed by someone and ran off leaving the victim body behind. I know it can't be a mugging as when I checked the victim over, all the valuables were still on the victim and in the victim handbag. one more thing!".

Sophia take's the rectangle torch and the chemical substance out of the case. Then pouring the substance in a line till the bottle was empty. She then turned the torch light on, that lit the alleyway up. With a purple light colour, that glowed onto the pathway. As Sophia pointed the torch toward the floor, where the chemical substance had been emptied. A glowing blueish line, within the purple light, reflected off the floor.

"That confirms the victim has been moved. Where you see the blueish line, within the purple light is the blood stain from the body being dragged".

Sophia looks at detective Jones as she speaks and replaces the torch and empty bottle back in the case.

"So do we have a name for the victim?".

Asked detective Jones

"Yes, you can see one of the pieces I pulled from the handbag was an ID card. Her name is Kayleigh Southan and she is twenty-six years old. Which also states on the ID card detail of where she lived".

Said Sophia, as she passed the detective Jones the evidence bag that contained the ID card, with the details of the victim name, age and address. So he was able to write down the information from the ID card for later and to have officers to check the address.

"Well as soon as we are done, I'll be sending an officer to that address stated on the ID card. to see if we are able to get in contact with a relative or friend. Who is able to identify the victim, as we need the positive ID. Even known we have evidence of the victim. We still need a positive to prove the victim is the person in question. If we don't get any luck at the address. I'll get the officers to knock around neighbours doors to see if the neighbour's know any other addresses of relatives or friends of the victim. That will, be all for now I will see you at the morgue later today".

Detective Jones passes the evidence bag with the ID card back to Sophia. Before he walked back to his vehicle, to head back to the police station. As Sophia watch him disappear into the distance and watched as he drive off. She places the evidence bag back onto the floor next to the triangle with the letter allocated to it. Sophia stood up and grabbed the camera out of the big case, to take pictures of the victim and evidence that was placed around the victim's body. By this time the rain had stop and the sky was becoming blue. Also, the gentle blowing wind became cold, with a sharp frosty breeze. When it hit Sophia's cheeks, it made her shiver now and again. Once finished taking pictures of the area and around the victim. She placed camera back in the case and picked the evidence and equipment up.

Placing everything into the case, locking the case with the number locks as she closed the lid. Then Sophia turned her head towards the two men standing by a van, they had arrived in. Who had been there for quite a while, waiting to retrieve the victim body to take back to the morgue.

Both men where standing there in their black suit and ties with white shirts on. The one on the left was a oldies chubby guy with grey hair on both sides of the head and flicked the hair from one side to the other so it would cover the bald spot with greenish brown eyes. The other was young tall and skinny man, that had short spiked brown hair with blue eyes that had a sharpness within them. The young man had a metal bed that was folded and a folded body bag, stuffed between the folded bed and the mans arm.

Giving the men the nod indicated Sophia was ready for them to collect the victim body. Either side of the men was an officer standing by the ribbon that closed the area off, from the public. Both of these officers were brothers and both looked alike as they were twins, with black hair and brown eyes. Both were slim and tall and well know for doing pranks at the police station. Also, they liked giving each other their own name, so the bosses would get confused who was who.

The two men in the black suits walked over to the victim that was laid out on the floor and unfolded the metal bed. Placing the body bag on top of the bed. One of the men unzipped the bag, while he did this he lowered the bed to the floor. So the victim could be placed in the body bag and then slid across onto the bed. Without having to pick up the body bag with the victim inside. Before strapping the body bag. They zipped up the victims body and strapped the bag onto the bed which had two straps, one at the top and one at the bottom of the bed. These were sealed across to prevent the body bag from sliding off the bed. The two men wheeled the bed to the back of the van and opened the back door of the van. Where they slid the metal bed onto the railing. Making the wheels of the bed fold inwards as the metal bed went into the van. So that the bed was able to slide into the van with the body bag still on the metal bed. By this time Sophia had packed up and was heading back to the police station, before going to the morgue. So Sophia could drop the evidence off and have the photo's developed down in the police station lock up. That the police station lock up can store the evidence and photo's they had developed for when the detective's are ready to analyze them for the case.

Chapter Two

THE LETTER

Detective Jones sat there in his office swinging backwards and forwards on his leather chair. Clicking the pen, while gazing at the computer screen. Thinking how to start and word the statement. He reached over and picked up the steamy hot coffee of his desk, that was positioned between the keyboard and phone. While sipping the coffee he takes a glance at the notebook on the other side of the keyboard. Which had been left open on the page of the notes, he had taken at the crime scene earlier.

The office was a small box room with a door that had square piece of glass, with detective Jones name printed in the centre of the glass. The room contained a desk next to the square window, with a view of the buildings across the other side of the main road. To dim out the noise from the busy road. The window was fitted with double glazing. On the desk contained an old computer monitor and a telephone. Just in front was a keyboard and a mouse that rested on a foam mat. Behind the monitor was a hole in the desk for the wires to go through, where the central processing unit was placed just underneath. Beside the computer was a chipped large mug that was used to rest pens and other office item. Either side of the leather chair was a set of three draws containing key locks, that the detective Jones never locked. Just by the door was a cabinet where the detective

Jones placed the case files. Which he locked all the time. On the other side of the cabinet just above. Was a large round plastic clock that had two hands, that stuck out and smily face as the back ground. The nose on the clock was hidden by the hands that showed the time. The office was also fitted with blue carpet tiles that had started to fade, as time went on. The walls of the office used to be white, that started to discolour from dirt and smoke over the years. It cause them to turn a yellowish.

Just as the detective started to type the statment out. The chief inspector Karl walked into the office. Holding a shoe box underneath his arm. Which contained a red ribbon tied around the box with a bow to give a presentable touch.

"This shoe box is addressed to you and was found on the reception desk, by one of the officers an hour ago. I have no idea who left it there for you. As you know the camera in reception area is still not working. So there is no way of telling who dropped the shoe box off. I thought I would drop the shoe box off personally as we need to talk".

While the chief inspector placed the shoe box onto the desk, in front of the detective Jones. The chief inspector moves forward, as he sits down in the chair. With his left elbow resting on the desk and his left hand resting underneath his chin. While one of his index finger gently pressed against his left cheek. He puts his thumb underneath the chin looking at the detective Jones as they talked. While detective Jones sat in his chair with both arms folded still holding the pen in his left hand.

The chief inspector was a tall slim man with brown eyes. Oval shaped glasses that rested on the bridge of his nose. The glasses had tinted glass in them with a thin black frame around the glass. That also had holes punched into the arms of the glasses. He had short brown hair with grey hair growing out of the sides, which was always kept short and tidy. With his brown suit and striped shirt. Two gold cuffs, containing a tiny diamond in the center of each gold cuff. Sealing the sleeves together on either side, of the shirt. A gold watch that was just above his left hand and a plain gold wedding ring on his finger. That had a tiny diamond in the centre. His tie was held neatly by a gold tie pin, which was clipped to the tie through the gap where the buttons go on the shirt. That the tie matched the colour of the suit. The brown shoes he had on, where shined that much you could see your own reflection in them as clear as day. The chief inspector was an ex-military man, who joined the police forces in his late eighties and moved up the ranks very quickly. Within two years of being at the police station. He was a very intelligent man, that made him strong minded and a very demanding person. He was the type of person that wanted things done on time and was always abrupt if things where late or not done the way, he wanted it done. He was a very strict person with a heart of gold. That always looked after his fellow workers and always took his fellow workers out every weekend for a pint down at the local pub.

"I have a new partner for you to help with this case. She has been transferred from another police station and she has just been promoted to detective, so I need you to show her the ropes. Look after this one. I can't keep finding you new partners all the time and try to be less short tempered. As this is why you are losing your partners. Because staff just can't stand working with you. Her name is Jessica O' Brien, known as detective O' Brien. This one will be a challenge for you. As she right down your street. She's not the type of person who will take your bullshit. Trust me she will give it back. Which is a good thing as both of you will get along with each other".

The chief inspector sat looking straight at detective Jones by giving that look, to say. "Screw this up and I have you by the balls. I mean it this time".

"I know I'm short tempered. But I try to work with these partners you allocate me. They can't do the job properly and it stresses me out that I have to carry these idiot. Which I end up having to do twice amount of work".

As detective Jones sat in his chair, staring away from the chief inspector. Holding his pen that he was clicking. That he held firmly in the palm of his hand causing it to started to sweat. Looking down at the floor, he was feeling awkward at that present moment in time.

"At least, give this detective a chance as you might be very surprised at what detective O' Brien is capable of doing. By the report I received from the other police station it was quite remarkable. Even I was shocked in what I had read. So I am telling you to change your attitude and work as a team. Your a good detective and always get results. Which make you one of the best detective's we have in this police station. This is why I am putting your name forward for my job when I retire at the end of the year, ok. You are going to be busy doing an NVQ level 4. As you need management training to be able to do my job. So that when you complete the NVQ you will be tested and passed by an assessor, before your interview. If all goes well you will be given the position as an acting chief inspector. Where I can train you for my job over the next six month while you are on probation. Just to let you know the NVQ is at the college. Where an assessor will train you one day a week from the college. He/she will come in to see you over a period of three months. Giving you paperwork to complete. I know this is short but I need you to pass and I know you are very fast in getting courses done as you have a very high score test rate during police college and when you was applying for the detective position. The NVQ must be completed by the target date. So you are able to sit for the test in the middle of May. If you pass the test you will be interviewed by the commissioner from Scotland Yard at the end of may, offering you the promotion. You will start the first of June as an acting chief inspector. On the six month period probation. After the six months you will have a meeting with me and the commissioner from Scotland Yard. By giving you the position of chief inspector or demoting you back to detective. Which means I have to stay till they can train and find a suitable candidate for my job. I believe in you and know you will do well in the six-months probation as you are my best detective who deserves the job. When applying for promotion you should get it. The appraisals given within the job and working over the years have been very good. The only thing is that could let you down is the way you are with others. Causing you to keep losing your partners, through your mood swings. I am giving you this last chance to prove to me and the commissioner who agree's with me. That you are able to work in a team and able to manage while working as part of a team. Giving you that important step towards the job. By moving up the rank within the police station. I would like to give the position to a detective within this station. Rather have one come from a different area. The job you will take on when you become chief inspector will require you to receive reports from staff. Then forward a copy of a report's on crimes that are solved and unsolved that week. Sending it to the senior officer who is the general manager. Know as the madam chief commissioner. The madam chief commissioner is the officer who run's the police stations in Lincolnshire and Yorkshire area's. Visiting once a week for a couple of hours to read the report that has been given on crimes during that week. The madam chief commissioner will go to the other station's to receive other reports on crimes. Expecting the crime rate on unsolved cases to be complete within the first month and to be lower than the solved cases. The madam chief commissioner will set a high rate of ninety five percent of cases to be solved. For this police station. We are just below that mark. Showing that you have solved over fifty percent of crimes for the Grimsby police station, out of the ninety-one percent. That includes the cases you help to solve in other departments of the police station. The madam chief commissioner will spend a day at Scotland Yard by passing the copy of the report. Onto the house of parliament and to the senior officer. Who the madam chief commissioner report to. So that estimate are kept over the year on report's of crimes. Putting crimes into their own categories. Then calculate to find out how many are solved and unsolved crime's with in the Lincolnshire and Yorkshire area's. You will receive a report of the percentage given on them figures and be reporting the figures to staff. In the monthly staff meeting. That same report will go to the house of parliament and a copy to the madam chief commissioner, senior officer. When the new year start's a report of the total year of crimes will be released to the media and public. Showing if crime's have gone up or down in these categories. Given a percentage figure and using last years figures to calculate the difference. Taking the figures from the crime rate. Placing them into each category. This gives a result that shows each crime will need to be looked at or put aside during that year. The percentage on each category will go onto a chart and pie chart. Which shows percentages over a period of so many years. It will then be decided by houses of parliament if the law changes or a new law is created for policies and procedures on crimes in the Lincolnshire or Yorkshire areas. By giving a new act to the law that has changed or new law created for that year. The madam chief commission will receive a report and sent a copy of the report. On any new law or if a law as been changed. You will then file a copy into the policy and procedures. Staff within police station will read, the new laws or laws that have been changed and sign it. This is what you will be required to know when you sit the test for your promotion. I will type up what I said to you and send a copy to you. Which will give you everything on running and controlling staff. Getting the most output within the police station. Having a good turnover through the year, low wastage. Having a low turnover of staff leaving and coming. Which will improving the profit margin. The information I give to you is for you to read and learn. This will prove you with understanding the knowledge and will help you pass the test. With the manager course, you will be taking, it will give you an understanding when answering the question. While doing the course I will take time in showing you the ropes before your promotion, so that it will give you more of chance when doing the NVQ_4 and passing the test. You will gain better knowledge, understanding and it will help you complete the course in good time. Also, it will give you the skills. As you learn the basic knowledge in management. While working with you a couple of hours one day a week. Out of my own time. You will be able to learn as you complete the course and work toward the main test before the interview. The reason is I want you to get this promotion. So don't let me down, when it comes to working as part of a team".

As the chief inspector put his strict face on and takes his voice up a level, to say.

"Not interested anymore about you having to take on double work. Just get on with the job and work with detective O' Brien as it will benefit you in the long run. Nothing more said that is the end of it. I don't want to hear anymore about it. Like I mentioned a number of time. I want to make sure it get's through to you, just don't let me down. I am putting all my chips on the table and taking a big gamble here on an employee who is able to go very far in the police force. If you pull your socks up and work with people instead of trying to do things by yourself. You might even make chief commissioner in the near future"

A few minutes later there was a heavy knock on the office door. The kind of knock that made the glass vibrate. As the chief inspector turned his chair to the side resting his left arm on the desk using his index finger tips to tap as the door opened. Detective O'Brien came towards the chief inspector. He moved his arm off the desk to shake her hand firmly and pointed in the direction of detective Jones.

"Hello, detective O'Brien how are you?. I would like you to meet detective Jones your new partner. Who you'll be working with and who will be showing you the ropes. For the next few months, detective Jones will be in charge of you. While you are on a six month probation period and I will end it one week early as I will have to take detective Jones under my wing if detective Jones gets the promotion. So that you are able to take on a new detective as your partner. Who will need training when they start as a detective. It will be a sergeant or team leader officer that works here or at another station. By training the officer for the promotion. To work in the detective department on probation over six months like you are doing now. Which is lucky for you as that means you will only be doing twenty-five weeks on probation not twenty-six weeks. After that you will be a detective same as detective Jones and up to that time you are working on probation. You will still be classed the same as a detective Jones and will be paid the same as a detective Jones. You are expected to turn up to work in plain clothes wearing a suit that you are dressed in. While training as a detective and when you become a detective. Also you can wear as much jewellery as you like as it looks good when doing stake outs. While keeping an eye on the criminals to make a mistake. Catching the criminals in the act while he/she is doing the crime. Before making arrested. This makes the criminals think you're just a normal person while sat in the car or walking around. Criminals will not expect you for being an undercover police officers when wearing normal clothes and lots of jewellery. The only time you not allowed to wear jewellery, is when you are interviewing the criminals to the crimes they had committed or interview the victim's or victim's family of the crimes that had been committed. Also, when visiting the morgue, transporting prisoners to other area's or crimes scenes that require criminal's to show where evidence can be found. As it always professional to look smart and wears the badge around your neck or show it by placing on the interview table. When visiting a criminals house, victims and family of victim's you must show your badge. Then putting it back in your pocket if it not around your neck. Never let the badge out of sight as it contains details that are required to protect you from becoming a victim of crime. If a criminal gets hold of the badge. It has been known in case's that crime that gets committed on motorways were victims get their vehicle pulled over thinking it the police, that are stopping them by an unmarked vehicle. That has flashing blue light, using a detective badge that been stolen. Making it easy for the criminals to do the crime that been committed, by just having normal clothes on. Instead of wearing a police officers uniform. This is why it is very important that you have your badge at all times. If you lose your badge. You have to report it within less an hour of know it has gone. Which you know and should know that from previous training courses you have been on. The reason I am telling you is with a detective badge it harder for the traffic police to find the criminal. The only way the traffic cop can find and stop the criminals is when the criminals are using the blue flashing light. Most victims will not remember the car plate number because of the trauma they have experienced by the crime that had been committed. Causing the victim to forget little important bits or they not released they been victim of crime that as been committed as they believed the criminals were detectives. When your probation is up you will attend appraisal with me and detective Jones who will discuss with you. Overall outcome on all aspect within your job role as a detective. Which we will give an answer to what we will decide to do. By keeping you as a detective or demoted you back to a sergeant base on the aspects of preformats. The job, how well you took control of the staff, cases and running of department within the police station. Each case you take on will be watched and monitor by detective Jones and occasionally will be working with you on the cases. Other than that detective Jones will be busy on many occasion as he will need to complete the paperwork that is required for him to finished on time. If detective Jones is busy there will be his ex-partner who is detective Towson that will be working with you while detective Jones is out. Detective Towson will be letting detective Jones know of any update on the case that is being dealt with at that present time. Over the period of six months. I am going by your skills used in the job. Watching you very closely by monitoring your performances that will give me a decision on the day you have your appraisal. The duties you have done over the past five years from the time you left police college has been excellent and the test scores you got was very high. above average when applying for higher ranks within the police job. Making you one of the top officer's from Cleethorpes Station. Which I received the report on you and was pleased with the results I read in the report. The reason for detective Jones not being there much is working towards to becoming an acting chief inspector who will be in charge when I am not here. As I will be having an early retirement and moving to Australia to my new house I pay for while I was on holiday in Queensland Austraila. Hopefully, detective Jones will make me proud and become the next chief inspector so you will be taken detective Jones place while he acting chief inspector. I trust you and feel you will be a detective in six-months just by that outstanding report I received before you came here. I have a good feeling you will be good for this promotion and think you will fly through the twenty five weeks with flying colours as you reminded me of detective Jones. Alway thirsty for more and completing cases in a short period of time. Over the couple of years I know detective

Jones, he has earned his promotion ten times over. I notice the report when you did the NVQ 3 you had completed the test above averaged and passing the NVQ 3 when you applied for a senior officer position. As a detective you are required to take charge of meeting with staff like sergeant. Team leader and police officers in the police station and work with the other detectives as part of a team. Also, you work as the murder investigator in the homicide department given you skills that you can be able to, pass on your skills once you become a qualified detective. After the probation period when you meet your new partner. As each detective's work along with a partner in different areas of crime so that you not all treading on each other feet and the case's are dealt with in a professional way. Which will not put too many detectives on one case and if the detectives are not busy in the department they are working which happens rarely. When they don't have any cases to work on. They can help with assassinating other detective's and will leave you and your partner to write up the report for me. You and your partner will receive reports from the detective's and officer's if new evidence come up or any information that you require. If you don't have any cases you would deal with the other detective's case's and give the report to the detective's that are dealing with that case. If you happen to come across any evidence or in formation that is vital. Which could solve that case and you will be noted down as a detective involved as part of the case in solving it. They will then forward a copy to me of the report so that the detective's working on the case will be kept informed and up to date with everything. The madam chief commissioner is a lady that come in from Scotland Yard and we call her mum when spoken to. Which you should already know who she is from your last police station. The commissioner comes in on Monday morning for a couple of hours. That like to see everyone working hard. So for them couple of hours you brief police officers and send the one not doing anything out on patrol in morning. Then make yourself disappear. If you have nothing to work on, get a unmarked car and just drive about keeping an eye on the officers and if any crime happens you will be notified by radio. when the commissioner has gone you will be ok to come back and as long as the paperwork has been filed and reports are done you can sit around. Why working on the evidence in your office just in case you might of miss something important till you have finished your shift. Only when I get the reports late or not completed reports. It annoy's me. The madam chief commissioner is very tough on staff when they are not completing the report. She will check everything to make sure it is done and on time. The madam chief commissioner will expect the crime rate on unsolved cases to be completed within the first month and does give leeway on case's that are lacking the evidence to complete. By setting a high rate of ninety five percent of cases to complete in any month. The rating we have are around ninety one point eight percent of solved case's, which is very good even though we are still not meeting the targets required. When I came here many years ago the targets were only in the seventy percent placing the target way below average".

She turned and walked around the right side of the desk once she had greeted the chief inspector and listened to what he had to say. Which was overwhelming as he had that much to say it was like having a class at the college. Taken in the vast amount of information made her forget what had been said. She could only take in bits of it, due to the time and as she was tired from lack of sleep. From being excited on starting her new promotion within her job. So while the chief inspector talked. She wrote in shorthand writing. The important things so she was able to check back on them in her own time. Keeping up to date on everything that would help her get through the probation period. While detective Jones sat in his chair, looking at detective O' Brien. Smiling ear to ear, thinking to his self how he will make it his task to work with detective O' brian. To become the best and looking to climb the ladder as he so badly wanted the higher ranking officer's job. Where he would be that much closer to his goal of leaving Grimsby. To take the rank of a chief commissioner at Scotland Yard. It was the job he alway's wanted even though he hadn't got the job yet as chief inspector. Detective Jones leans forward placing his pen onto the table. Holding out his hand that was sweaty and very warm from the pens being held that firmly causing the palm to heat up. He grabs her hand, she grab his hand. Shook it a few time and then pulling it away sliding it down the side of her trousers to wipe away the sweat that transferred onto the palm of her hand. Standing in front of detective Jones as she looked at him and began to speak. While she was slowly wiping her hand without the chief inspector or detective Jones noticing what she was doing.

"Hi, it is a pleasure to meet you detective Jones and to be working with you on this case, hopefully many more cases in time to come".

"Yes detective O' Brien, it's a pleasure to meet you in person. Hopefully we will be working together through your probation and when I get my promotion. I will be able to be happy with the cases that you will or maybe be doing when I become chief inspector. I'll be the one that will show you the ropes of the job and working together as part of a team".

As detective Jones leans back into the chair facing in the direction of detective O'Brien as she stood thinking how long this will take so she could wash her hand that contained the sweat. Which made her feel dirty from knowing that she had someone else's sweat on it. Has detective Jones was sweating in both palms of his hands. feeling very nervous of the chief inspector. While he sat there with arms crossed and legs crossed. Watching and observing what was being said. Detective Jones knew in his head that he was being watched. He looked straight into detective O'Brien eyes as he sat there for a second or two, then switching eye contact at the chief inspector while feel awkward.

Detective O' Brien was a very attractive woman, with light brown skin and lips. she had dark brown beautiful eyes, with medium dark eyelashes. Nails that had been professionally done. The hair was long and dark that was straighten for a professional look and she was a well-spoken person who would tell you straight if she was not happy with anything. Her gold earrings that dangle down in both ears with round and thin shape. with two gold studs in both ears that had a light purple stone that covered the front of the gold studs. Glittered multiple colours of light. Which moved around the office walls as the sunlight beamed off the earrings. Detective O' Brien had a white top that was covered by her black suit jacket and trouser to match the jacket. Also, black shoes that had a fashionable look to them. Wearing jewellery on both hands and neck, make her look very smart and intelligent.

At that point the chief inspector spoke before standing up and leaving the office.

"I will leave you two to get to know each other better and to get on with the case. I expect a report on my desk by tomorrow at nine in the morning of what you have on the case so far. Don't be late with the report or I'll have both of you by the scruff of the necks. So detective Jones you better bring detective O' Brien up to date on the case as I expect two reports. one from you and the other from detective 'O' Brien. Understand detective's".

With both of them nodding their heads at the same time. While looking at the chief inspector has he walked out of the office closing door behind him. Detective Jones sat in his chair glazing into the computer screen. Waiting for detective O' Brien to say something first. As he was the type of person who expected his partner to ask for the information without him having to think for his partner.

"So tell me what is the case we are looking at and is there anything you want me to do in the meantime".

Speaking in a low tone voice, detective O' Brien stood there nervous as it was her first day in a new police station and being promoted to detective in the job. She didn't know what to expect from the job or what the job entailed. As she was given the promotion with the new location just twenty-four hours ago. Told she be trained by her new partner. Detective O' Brien only knew detective Jones by name and face. She didn't know anything about him. What he was like to work with and what the detective job role involved. Has it was new to her, even know she work with other detective's in Cleethorpes. Detective O' Brien never know what they did as she was alway out or in the station typing out reports and statement then passing the report on to the detective who was dealing with the case at that moment. She had a general idea from the information give by the chief inspector. Knowing the information was not like put it into practices and doing the job. Detective Jones managed to shake his self out of the gaze that he was in. While turning his head away from the computer screen. Looking straight at detective 'O' Brien as she sat down in the chair. Detective Jones picks his pen up off the desk and started to swing his chair from side to side, holding the pen with the clicking bit tapping against his bottom lip. He began to speak.

"The case so far is".

Glancing at the notebook every so often.

"At one thirty a.m. I arrived at the crime scene at the alleyway of Freeman Street Market. Where a young woman was found murdered in a sitting position. Leaning to the right side. Which was approximately half way to three quarters of a way down the alleyway. We retrieved from the victim handbag an ID card. That contained a picture and information of the victim. Her name is Kayleigh Southan. She is twenty-six years old and also states on ID card where she lives. The reason for keeping the handbag is it was next to the victim. Plus it can be tested for evidence and the ID card is it contains personal detail that we require. There was other items in the hand bag which had been removed like makeup and a purse that contained cash, bank card, credit card, membership cards and other cards. These items will be handed back to the family. After they have signed for the evidence we keep and the item family will take with them. Load of empty sweet wrappers, paper which was no value so it was disposed of. Tablets, about four different ones and I know about one or two of them the others don't know as most of the tables wasn't in a box. These have or will be sent to pharmacy to be correctly named and destroyed after a week. Two forms will be filled out with the names of the tablets. One will come to police station and the other will be sent by fax before autopsy is done today. The other document fax is the medical history. To eliminate any non-evidences while the autopsy is being done. Has it important to get the correct evidence from the corpse. The crime scene officer arrived at the scene at two a.m. The victim had her hair and skin removed of the crown part of the head, with marking on the skull. The skull appears to be showing where the hair and skin used to be, with zig-zag around the edges of the skin that had been left. Which the crime scene officer said the murderer must have used a jagged sharp object to cut the hair and skin from the head. Also, the killer is left-handed and due to the force of the way the murderer sliced the skin and hair off. Caused the brian fluid to leak from the right ear. The victim also had blood seeping though her dress from the stomach. which the crime scene officer cut a hole across the stomach area of the dress to find out where the blood was coming from. Showing part of the stomach. Where the victim's stomach had been punctured by a sharp object. Maybe the same object used for cutting the hair and skin of her head. The crime scene officer be able to give us more detail, when she examines the victim body back at the morgue. She also did a outline of the victim body. Bagged all the evidence and took pictures of the victim and evidence within the crime scene area. Then place the evidence and camrea into the lock-up at the police station. Where all the evidence get stored. The storage room of the lock-up is down in the cellar part of the building and the staff who work in lock-up will develop the photos from the crime scene. For when we ready to sign the evidence and photo's out. I left the scene at four a.m. and was informed that the body of the victim was bagged and taken to morgue around five thirty a.m. After the crime scene offier had finished everything she needed to do in that area. At six a.m. I received a memo with the date and time as the reference number that is used to get the evidence and photos out of the lock-up. The two officers at scene reopen the area at six fifteen a.m. After everyone had left the crime scene area and arrived back at the police station at six forty five a.m. I called the two officers from the crime scene and a lady officer into the office at seven a.m. and sent them to the address which was on the ID card. To see if the victim as a family or friends living at the same address. If the victim lives by her self or no one in. I've told the officers to knock on the neighbours doors to find out if they know of the victims family or friends whereabouts. So we are able to get in touch with a family or friends who can identify the victim body. Even known we have an ID card with the victim name on and picture of the victim. We still have to get a positive identification of the victim from a family or friend so it can be logged down in the case. Also, it will help the family and friends of the victim. To be able to put their minds at ease, by coming to term with the loss of their loved one. The reason I sent lady officer with the two men officers because the women officers are better dealing with the emotion. When the officers inform a family or friend of the loss of their loved one and when they identifying the victim body back at the morgue. The lady officer will be comforting the family or friend while going through this sad time. As it can be hard and emotional for the family or friend who get informed and having to identify the victims body. Just the shock of hearing the news would make the family or friend fill drained of finding out what happened to their loved one. So by giving them the support and comforting them would help. Before you and the chief inspector Karl came into the offices I was just about to start my statement on the case. Which I need to get finish before ten thirty a.m. today. As we have to visit the morgue for an autopsy to be done and for any new evidence that we don't know about at the moment. The family or friend should have identified the victim and left the building by the time we arrive at the morgue for the autopsy. That all I know at the moment so far on the case. Which you can read in your spare time once the statement is completed".

As detective Jones sat there in his leather chair, fiddling with his pen. While speaking to detective O' Brien.

"So what do you need me to do, while I wait till it's time to leave for the morgue".

Said detective O' Brien

"Ok, I need to get this statement done as I only have about an hour to finish it. Once done it will help you to catch up with the speed of the case and give you an idea of what's happened so far in the case. So while I do the statement just pick me up a bacon sandwich and a coffee from canteen please, thank you".

Detective O'Brien pull out the notebook and starts to write down the direction in the notebook. While detective Jones tell her, he uses is left hand to point in the direction.

"Which is out this door turn right, down the corridor. Through the double doors you used this morning. Go through the reception and use the card you was given or code if you not got a card yet, as it the same code number to the door on the opposite sided. Follow the corridor around and the canteens just through the double doors. On the way back after you have dropped off the sandwich and the drink off. I would like it if you would do me this favour by just going to the lock-up and signing the evidence and photos out of the lock-up as we have to stick them on the board. In the investigation room that we been given for this case. Just go out that door and down the corridor, take a left. Then right and down the stairs. At the bottom of the stairs you arrive at a double doors. The code to the double doors is zero, one, four, two. Go through the double doors and there will be an officer in the room behind the safety glass. Which separate the store room. Tell the office that you need to collect the evidence and photos. Reference number\zeroseven\zero one\two thousand and fourteen\ zero, five, four, five. The officer will bring the evidence and photos to you. Which you sign for. Also, must write down the number thats on your ID badge next to your name and signature, so there's a log of who has the evidence and photos. I give you this memo I have in my pocket. It as the details of the reference number on it. That be all for now".

As detective Jones sat in his chair. He places his right hand in between the jacket and shirt. Pulling the memo out of his left top pocket of the shirt. Which was a yellow piece of paper. That was delivered by an officer from the lock-up department of the police station. Around eight a.m. After Sophia had dropped the evidence and camera off at the lock-up. The officer then logged the date and time of the evidences and camera being put into storage placing evidence into the cream colour box with lines on one side and camera into a plastic bag. Printing two stickers out and placing them into the box and plastic bag. Then sending one into a room full of boxes placed in order of dates and times. That contain evidence of other cases and passing the plastic bag to the officer who developed films. Once developed the pictures will go into the same box as the evidence. By using the evidence that came in as a date and time for a reference number, will make it easy to find.

"May I ask, does sir required milk and sugar with his drink".

As she stood up, on the other side of the desk looking down at detective Jones. While waiting to receive an answer.

"Milk and two sugars, I have not got time for this so would you just do what I asked for. I got to get on with this statement".

As he raises his voice, while sitting in his chair given detective O' Brien the look of authority as he turned his head away from the computer screen.

"Ok, but you didn't have to be like that".

As Detective O' Brien said sulkily as she turns to walk out the office and closed the door behind her. Speaking quietly under her breath saying. "You just wait, your time will come". Which detective Jones did not hear what she had said as the closed the door behind her.

Detective Jones sat in his chair rocking back and forwards staring at the shoe box with the red ribbon tied around it. Thinking about his new partner. Which was not about the job that he needed to complete but about having a partner that he had to work with. That he would rather work on his own as it was the only way he knew. He didn't have a problem with her or dislike her it was just that he worked better by his self and when he had a partner before it was like he was carrying his partner and that was why he was having second thoughts about detective O' Brien. The only thing was he wanted the chief inspector job. So he knew that he had to work with her as the chief inspector was retiring at the end of the year. Nothing even crossed his mind, about opening the box or even starting the statement. As he sat there lost in his own world, not been able to get away from his thinking. After a few minutes later. Like good five minutes detective Jones turned and started to type the statement out. During that time detective O' Brien pop in and drop off the coffee and bacon sandwich that detective Jones had asked for. Placing the sandwich down hard on the desk that made a bang as the plate touched the service of the desk saying. "There you go sir" as detective O' Brien walks out and close the door to the office behind her. Which did not help detective Jones with his temper and the statement. Causing him to forget where he was on the statement and he couldn't think with the distraction of detective O' Brien coming into the offices. Slamming the sandwich down the way she did and leaving the offices. He sat there thinking he will be getting detective O' Brien by giving her a good talking to. This was not the type of partner he wanted as he was stressed with her. As soon as he gets the time to bring the subject up again. It took a while to get back to where he was on the statement, once detective Jones had finished the statement he save the file under case number 247 on the computer and printed two copies out. Where he placed one of the copies of the statement into a brown paper folder and marked just at the right corner of the folder with the case number. Placing the copy into the cabinet, then popping next door, where detective O'Brien new office was and placed it onto the desk next to the computer. The layout of the office was the same as his. The only differents was it didn't have her personal belonging. The office looked like there was no one still using it the only different was the name had changed on the glass of the door which detective Jones never took notice. As it was put on the door a couple of days ago. So that detective O'Brien could view the report and when needed she always had a copy in her filing cabinet.

Detective Jones sat back down and glanced at the clock. Letting out a sigh of relief knowing that he had quarters of an hour left before having to go to the morgue. Then detective Jones glanced at the shoe box with the red ribbon around it. That was still sitting on desk unopened. So he decided to open the shoe box to see what someone had got him. It was quite strange that someone had sent him a shoe box with a red ribbon attached around it. As detective Jones felt shocked and emotional from receiving a gift. He never had anything given to him like this before. Sitting looking at the shoe box. Detective Jones could only think that it was the woman who he was friend with. Which he was also having benefits with, when he spending time with her. Detective Jones was the perfect man.

Showing his love and attention. By making the woman feel like a million pounds. Maybe it was the twins officers playing one of their pranks on detective Jones. Like them officers were the type you could never get angry with. Just made you laugh most of time or was it the new detective O' Brien who could be a bit of a joker or given me a gift to welcoming a long and good partner within the job. By sending detective Jones a shoe box all he could think was it could be a joke in the box or nothing. Just an empty box address to him. Detective Jones lend over and pick up his cold bacon sandwich that had being sitting there for a while and took a bite out of it, as the grease spread around his mouth. He replaced the sandwich back on the plate before he grab the ribbon and pulling it. Loosing red ribbon of the shoe box. Suddenly the blood drained from detective Jones face sending his face that white. He stood up, trembling with his eye wide open from shock. As he slowly slides the top lid of the box. Making him jerk back suddenly, nearly choking on the half eaten sandwich that he was still chewing on. He swallowed that fast it stopped him from taking a breath for a split second. Knocking the cold coffee over with his arm as he suddenly jerked backwards. Detective Jones stood there for a while. Then quickly picked up the receiver of the phone, dialling the number as his hands trembled with sweat. Waiting for an answer on the other end of the line. Still leaving the cold coffee to run off the edge of the desk onto the floor. Which was making a puddle of coffee as it dripped off the edge of the desk onto the floor.

"Goodmorning the morgue how can I help".

As a voice came across the receiver from the other end.

"Yyeeessss!!, yes this is detective Jones I need to speak to Sophia straight away, thissss is a very important matterrrrr".

As detectve Jones speaks with a scared and worrying voice, by this time the sweat slowly runs of his forehead. While detective Jones stood waiting for Sophia to answer on the other receiver, at the other end of the phone line.

"Hello detective Jones what did you need me for?, I will be seeing you in about half an hour".

Looking very puzzled in the face, Sophia knew detective Jones was coming to the morgue in just over half an hour.

"Can'tttt waitttt, right err I think. No, forget being their in an hour as I have the missing hair and skin in front of me. It seems that there is a letter left on top of a plastic bag containing the hair and skin, that has been placed inside a shoe box with a red ribbon tied around the outside of the shoe box. The shoe box was addressed to me, by only having my name and police station written on the lid of the shoe box. Saying to detective Jones, Grimsby police station in big letters that had been traced out onto the lid of the shoe box. To prevent the handwriting from being used as evidence. Left by a person that no one saw, leaving the shoe box on the reception desk. The only thing is that the camera in reception went down yesterday for some unknown reason. I wonder if this person had something to do with that cameras in reception. To stop me from being able to see who this person was, who had left the shoe box. Another thing how does this person know I've taken the case?. For this person to sent the evidence to me and how does this person know I'll be back from London to take the case?. The shoe box has been sat on my desk in the offices for quite a while before i decided to open it. I assume the bag in the shoe box is containing the smell so that's why I left the shoe box sitting there in front of me and didn't open it earlier as I assumed it was a gifted from someone. Till I open the lid of the shoe box and got the biggers shock of my life."

By this time the frustration of the shock, made the detective words come out wrong"

"Well you need to bring the shoe box with the new evidence in for me to take a sample and examine for further evidence".

With a quite excited feeling, Sophia knew that a big evidence had turned up. Which could help the case out, by finding a mistake that the murderer could have missed when sending the shoe box into the police station. Why do this? Does the murderer want something or does the murderer want to be known for that murder?

"Oooookkk, Sorry still in a bit of a shock was not expecting to find something like that. Also the feeling that the murderer knew who I am before we have released it to the press. It is like the person is studying the whole thing before deciding the next move when murdering the victims. Just thinking about it how long has this person has been watching and studying me?. To know that I was to be back in time to take this case.".

As detective Jones stood there with the receiver next to his ear. Thinking all different thoughts. As he repeats his self when talking to Sophia on the other end of the line.

"Detective Jones pull yourself together and bring the shoe box to me. This is not like you, well I have known you a long time and you have seen worse than this. So snap out of it and I will see you when you get here ok".

Putting on a strong voice as Sophia speaks to detective Jones. Hoping this would help him to snap out of his panic attack he was having. As sophia had seen this happen so many time when an officer falls into a panic attack. By letting it destory their career. The officer losing all ability to carry on with their duty and unable to proceed with the career. Sophia didn't want that to happen to her friend who sophia wanted to take the relationship that much further. Sophia had fallen in love with detective Jones and was starting to get fed up with the benefit she was getting with him. Sophia wanted more, not the love making that she was having here, there and everywhere. No, Sophia wanted everything, to be married, another kid if it was to happen and to live with detective Jones for the rest of Sophia lifetime. But every time Sophia mentioned she wanted to take the relationship to the next step. Detective Jones would change the subject by talking about something else. Which did hurt Sophia, it was like the feeling of having your heart ripped out and stamped on till there was nothing left of your heart. Like the detective Jones didn't even know that Sophia cries herself to sleep at night. Even when detective Jones laid next to Sophia, holding his hand across the chest of Sophia body with both their naked bodies touching each other. Still Sophia cared that much about detective Jones. She had to find a way to help him out of the panic he was having. The only way She knew of helping detective Jones out of his shock was talking and reassuring him. That he was worrying about nothing and that he would be fine. So it wouldn't make detective Jones go off the rails. Like Sophia had seen so many time in her career.

"Ok give me a second to sort my head out and I will be there as soon as I can. I need to read this letter and hold a meeting with my staff before I come down to the morgue. I will be running late. I'll give you a ring. To let you know that I am on my way. Ohh yeah I got a new partner who is on the case with me. I have to bring her with me to the morgue as well. Her name is detective O'Brien".

As detective Jones mentioned that he was bringing her. A feeling of jealousy came over Sophia. The feeling hit her like a ton of bricks. Even though it was work only between detective Jones and detective O'Brien. It was knowing another woman was being in detective Jones life. Yes it might be just a partner in the job. But knowing detective Jones was spending time in detective O' Brien company and the situation of them being friends with benefits put Sophia into a feeling she had lost for a while. Which suddenly hit Sophia at that moment in time. Like Sophia got from a person she knew year ago. She was with, who used to sleep around all the time. That same horrible feeling went through Sophia. When the words came out "I have to bring her and her name is detective O' Brien". This made Sophia eyes water with no way to stop them. As the tears ran down the cheek of Sophia's face. Sophia quickly wiping the tears away with her arm. In the way Sophia didn't care if detective Jones assumed that she was being selfish. As time was passing by in Sophia life and Sophia didn't want to be living a life that she had been doing. Sophia wanted her whole life to be that princess and have that dream wedding that hasn't come yet. Which seem to fade away slowly as the year passed bye. Two kids by the father that she lost to a fire and Sophia never wanted that to happen in their life. To see her kids never knowing their dad. Made Sophia hates herself everyday for having the life she lived. Yes Sophia was happy for having the kids. But didn't intended to bring both up on her own. She wanted to have both parents in her kids lifes.

"Ok see you soon".

Slamming the receiver down that hard made the phone leave the side for a split second before merging with the side again. Detective Jones quickly sorted his head out and pulled out plastic gloves and some plastic evidence bags for him to put the evidence in. Detective Jones made sure that he got one large evidence bag, so he could seal the shoe box in it with the hair and skin sample. Still inside the shoe box and a small one for the letter. Detective Jones carefully pulled the letter out of the shoe box. Placing it into the evidence bag. So he could read what it said and to prevent any damaged to the evidence. Detective Jones laid the letter on the desk neatly so the letters could be seen through the evidence bag. Before doing this he dialed down to reception to ask them to located his partner and to get detective O' Brien to the office as soon as possible. As Detective O' Brien walk in while forgetting to knock. Standing there in the middle of the room. She became very surprise in what she saw and quite intriguing that the evidence in the shoe box where sat for a long time before discovering that they were very important evidence to the case. As detective O' Brien holds the rest of the evidence from the crime scene in her hand. That the crime scene officer had dropped off previously at the lock-up. She Let's go of the box that contained evidence onto the middle of the floor and walked over to the desk where detective Jones was lent over looking at the letter in front of him. Detective O' Brien, does the same on the opposite side of the desk so that both their heads were nearly touching each other. Detective Jones switches his keyring light on, as the light on the keyring would bring up any blood or hand prints left on the letter. As he shines the light onto the evidence bag that contains the letter he notices only smudges on the edges of the letter. Which had being written out by some sort of ink onto the paper, they both started to read it.

"Hello, detective Jones or shall I just call you Chris,

Yes I will call You by your first name. I hope you were inspired by the artwork I left for you to find, no not right. Had to deal with, much better may I say. Hope that you didn't get too wet this morning. Especially when taking time to have a smoke. But I believe I had the best view ever. Watching you do your work not forgetting to clean away my art. Yes it was most beautiful work I ever did especially while listening to the most relaxing music. It didn't help that she had to scream while being tied up and had to have her mouth stuff with a cloth. It ruined the music a bit. But I can say the feeling I got looking into her scared eyes before they went as cold as ice. Was like the best thrill I got in my life. I can say it was better, much better than sex. Well getting back to business. As I don't want to let you know all my dirty secrets now or do I. Oh by the way I thought you could do with that hair I sent to you. So you can cover that patch on your head and maybe you can take that hat off you wear. Because I must say it doesn't suit you that much only joking!. It a trophy for you so that everyone know of my beautiful artwork.

Getting to the point, here some clues?

As I sit there while my kids sleeping in bed, watching the soaps. This is the end that has come for me. As I see my life passing away. First the fear, then the rope marks, following with a sharp pain. Now it is time to close my eyes and as I walk through as a spirit in time. I'll watch as my kids get a pleasant surprises. When they awaken to find their single mum passed away on the carpeted floor, with the tv still playing to itself. You have two days to find where I live, one adult, two kids in a house thats opposite aroundabout somewhere near Grimsby but not too far from town. Maybe Cleethorpe or maybe not and has three rooms to sleep in. So where am I tick, tick and tick the clock strikes again.

So there you go the clue has started to go. Will you make it or will you not make it and let her go. Two days you have no more, no less. So work it out or not as she has less than a couple of days to live or die. You only can be the one who decides her fate. As dinner apporaches. I hunger for the meat she contains near her stomach. Down below

I cut the meat out and fry meat for my lunch. Taste of the meat will give me the taste for more.

So who am I?

Your sincerely
Wait for you to give me a name
A name that I will live up to
By getting well known by others

P.S. My name is an old indian story, not too look too far as the hair will give you the clue to my name and I will be known for years as the murderer who made the 10 'o' clock new. While making my art go on and on. Ha Ha Ha!!!!

Chapter Three

THE MEETING

The footsteps echo down the corridor. Followed by the turn of a handle. With a squeaking sound as the door open.

"Quiet!"

As everyone stopped talking and looked straight ahead.

"Right, I want you all to get your notebooks out and write down everything I tell you. Today I received a parcel that contained contents of case 247. Also within the parcel was a note which the murderer as gave us a clue on the next victim. This means we only have less than forty-eight hour to work the clues out. Preventing the next victim being murdered and that may help us bring the murderer to justice".

As detective Jones stood by the board within the room. Stood Next to him to the right was detective O' Brien. With twelve officers sat in three row of four in front of the detectives. Just in between the detectives and office was two desks put together.

The room was long and narrow and had a white board on the wall which was filled information from case 247. Leaving space in the middle of the board for information to write down. Above the board was a square black clock and at the back of the room was folded chairs that rested against the walls. Beside a table that contained a boiler position on the left edge of the table. To the right side of the table was plastic cups and stuff for making a drink with. Two big windows that beamed light into the room with shades in each end of the windows. The floor had blue tile carpets and half of each wall was blue on the bottom half and cream on the top half.

Detective Jones picked the black marker for the board and starts to write as he talked.

"At one thirty this morning I attended a crimes scene of a victim found in the alleyway of Freeman Street Market. What do we have so far on the case. We have victim number one. Sex female, name is Kayleigh Southen, age twenty-six, location Freeman Street Market, place of murder unknown, how she was murdered unknown".

Turning around as he looks at the officers and said.

"I mean unknown on where she was murdered. The victim was dragged and found outside of Freeman Street Market, down an alleyway. There was abrasions on feet and scratched on the back of the shoes. This shows the victim had been moved from another area. The crime scene officer confirmed the blood stain which showed up from the chemical test. Showed the victim had not been murdered in that area. One, there was not enough blood in the area for the murder to take place. Two, the blood stains were straight with lots of curves in them. This was caused by the body as it was dragged as the body left a blood trail on the floor. Which meant the victim was dragged after being murder, to the crime scene area. The murderer might have been disturbed or left for the victim to be found. As he/she was watching. This means all people that were questioned in the area. While standing there watching and the person who found the victim. Could be the subject of the murder. I will need the two brothers Jake and George Officers Allen to go to the homes of the people that was questioned this morning at the crime scene. To ask some more question about the murder at the crime scene. Also to look around the subject house or flat as you might come across some evidence of the murder. That could lead convicting the subject in question. The murderer could be living close by or used a vehicle to move the body. Then dragged the body from the vehicle. I need Heather officer Stockwell and Steve officer Finch to go to houses and flats in the area of the crime scene and do the same as the other two officers, So we are able to limit out any possibilities that the murderer could be living in the area".

The woman officer Heather had light ginger hair, neatly held back. With hair clips and rolled into a ball at the back, held by a hair grip. Her light sharp blue eyes and eyebrows that were hard to see. With red lipstick and dark eye shadow that made her eyelashes look longer than they were.

The man officer was a short person, very well built. He had a musclebound body that just about fitted the uniform. Brown eyes and a moustache, that was that short you could mistake it for stubble and the same as detective Jones on the head only showing the bald patch. The skin was tanned with wrinkles appearing on his head as he stood up straight. With his fat head and flat nose that spread across his face.

Detective Jones carried on talking.

"Maybe she was murdered at the place, where the victim was attacked. I do know from the report from the officers who went to her address there was no sign of any evidences stating the victim was murdered in the house. Also the family has been notified and the lady officer is still with them, at this moment. Till the body has been identified by the family and an autopsy as been done. The crime scene officer is unable to pass family the information needed. For the family to inform the department of birth, marriage and death. So that certificate is ready for the victim to be laid to rest. Once everything is done and the information passed on. The crime scene officer will release the body to the undertakers that the family requested. How she died, we will know when autopsy has been done and report from autopsy is been given to me".

As detective Jones turned around as he pointed at the officers who were given the jobs. Turning back to the board to carry on writing while talking.

"Right back to what we know, on the murder of the victim. I know that the victim had her hair and skin removed which later found it's way to my desk. Within the shoe box that had the red ribbon tied around. The skin and hair will be tested when I arrive at the morgue for the autopsy. To see if it fits into the crown of the victm's head and to make sure that it matches the victm's skin and hair. I opened the shoe box around nine forty-five a.m. The box contained a letter addressed to me. That revealed evidence to the murder of the victim. I have underlined all evidence on the photocopied letter. which I copied a few moments ago. The real letter will be going with the shoe box and the evidence. To be studied for fingerprints or foreign bodies. That you all be able to take the time to look at when we are done here before leaving. The information containing on the letter will be given. How she was tied up around the arms and legs to prevent the victim from moving. The murderer also placed a cloth within her mouth, so the victim was unable to scream. So that he/she was able to listen to music playing in the background. While he/she was murdering the victim. Also stated the person was going to remove something from just below the stomach area. Which the person could have taken something already with the first victim. As she had blood around that area of the stomach. One more thing on this, that I would also like to mention. He/she was taking this part of the body and eating it that make this person a cannibal. Which means we are not dealing with an amateur. This person is one sick individual, who plans their attack before he/she murders the individual. By making them their victim. As the murderer watches or studies the victim and knowing the detective who will be dealing with the crime. Which is me at this present time. Involving the victim into some sick game the murderer wants to play. As the murderer knew where to send the shoe box and who to send it to means he/she must have known I was dealing with the murder case and properly studying me too. I believe the person is very intelligent when planning the murder. For a number of days before going ahead with the crime to take the victims life. By gathering information on the victim and information contained in the letter. Shows that he/she has met me in person or collected information on me and knows who I am. The reason is the murderer knew me by my first name, not as detective Jones. Knowing I had been away for a bit and when I arrived back. As I only arrived back yesterday. Knowing that I would be dealing with the case and the very important thing is he/she had been watching me. While dealing with the victim in Freeman Street Market".

Detective Jones turned around for a few second while waiting for officers to catch up as they copied down notes in their notebooks. Turning back and carry on writing, as he talked.

"Carrying on, we do know that the murderer is left handed by the way he/she had cut into the head and there was brain fluid dripping from the right ear. Where the brain had caused pressure. Causing the right ear to fill up with the brain fluid and popping when the skin in the ear is unable to stretch anymore. The brain fluid then seeped out of ear as the murderer cut into the head. Removing the hair that also still had skin attached to it. When being separated from the head. Which was the crown of the head. That showed teeth marks on the skull. Showing that the murderer had used some sort of sharp object that had serrated edges. As he/she removed the skin and hair from the victim. Also leaving the remaining skin around the skull to have jagged end. Showing that the murderer knew how far to cut into the skin as he/she never cut into the skull just scraped the surfaces".

While speaking about what the murderer had done. Detective Jones stopped writing. Turning back to the board and pointing with the pen at the items that were placed around the board where he had written in the middle.

"Evidence, pictures of items found on the victim and in her handbag. Two new pictures were taken not long ago one of a shoe box with a red ribbon. One of a bag containing hair and skin of the victim. A photocopy of the letter to me from the person who murdered the victim. This is important I want you to take notes of what I write down and evidence. We have at this present time. Including information from the letter. The murderer likes to write in riddles. On the letter it states, the person has been watching me for sometime. So we need to keep our eyes and ears open as you never know if something pops up or you might hear anything relating to the murder. The person calls it artwork and by the sound of it, they find it enjoyable in a sexual way. The person likes to listen to music as he/she take the life of the victim and could be buying music or downloading music. So check all computers. Cassie Officer Detriot and Wayne Officer Bagshaw. I need you to check all shops and music shops in the local area. If anyone has been buying relaxing music in the past few days. Check the cameras while you are there, never know something might give us some leads".

Cassie known as officer Detriot was a dark skinned man, six foot tall and medium build. Dark Black short curly. Hair braided back with dark brown eyes. That spoke english with a Jamaican accent. With a beard that started beneath his bottom lip, down to beneath the chin and the side of his sideburns came down to the jaw bone on both sides of his face.

Wayne, officer Bagshaw was an oldish man with grey hair. He was tall and stocky built with a beer belly that hung over his trousers. With hazel brown eyes. Skin that had reddish areas, with only a couple of years left before retirement.

"Getting to the clues. That was given to me in the letter. We are looking for a single mum with two children in a house that is by a roundabout. The house is three bedrooms and just outside Grimsby. The only thing that got me is it not far from town this could be a key to the next victim whereabouts. Also he/she said maybe in Cleethorpes or maybe not. We have to work this out as we only have between thirty-six to forty hours. Give and take to work out where the next victim lives. I need everyone to put your heads together and come up with results within the next's twenty-four hours so we can get this person before they strike again. So give me results guys. Julie officer Rose and Kelly officer Thorton. I need you to go to the council and pull all the records of women who are single with two children in houses that are opposite aroundabouts, in Grimsby and Cleethorpes areas".

Julie officer Rose had brown hair tied back in a ponytail. That was clipped onto the top of her head. Brown eyes with light skin. With a very fit figure and a bum that stuck out and breasts that were double dee's that alway's had men whistling at her while out in her normal clothes.

Kelly officer Thorton was an english chinese woman, married to an english man. She had dark black hair with a chinese babble that held the hair roll into a ball on top of her head, with dark brown eyes. She was very slim, tall and very attractive. She spoke perfect english and was able to talk chinese from a very young age.

Detective Jones carried on talking.

"I take it that the sample of hair and skin is to let us know that this person did the murder. I have decided to call this person the Scalp Slayer. So we are looking for the Scalp Slayer murderer. The rest off you that I have not given jobs to do, Emma Officer Bells, Vincent officer clapton, Rob officer Wilkinson and Ben officer Simon. You will all work together by working the riddle out while me and Detective O' Brien attend the morgue for the autopsy. Does anyone have any questions. Idea of anything that could help with case 247"?.

Emma, officer bells was a short chubby woman with black hair brushed back into a ponytail and a chubby face. She was very good looking and alway's loved to have a laugh. Sharp blue eyes with long eyelashes.

Vincent, officer Clapton was a scottish man with ginger hair, bushy eyebrows. He was clean shaven meduim build. Hazel green eyes. Still had a very strong scottish accent when speaking. he had only been in Grimsby a couple of years.

Rob, officer Wilkinson was a type of ladies man and loved chatting up women when out or talking about ladies he had picked up to his friends. He was a man who looked younger then what he was. With dark hair and pretty face. Skinny and tall. He never had any rings on, just a gold necklace with a cross on it.

Ben, officer simon was the quiet type and never said much. He was medium build with short hair that was spiked up into the middle of his head like a mohican. Blue eyes and clean shaven.

"What age group we looking for sir?".

Office Wilkinson shouted out.

"Not known at this time, probably ages thirty to fifty".

Said detective Jones

"Is the person white, coloured or mixes sir?".

Offices Heather shouted out.

"Not known as It could be anyone from English, Irish, Welsh, Scottish or someone from another country and any colour".

Detective Jones speaks out.

"What profession are we looking for sir?."

As officer Vincent calls from the back row seat.

"Well any from Doctor, Vet, Chef or a Professor. Going by the letter and how the victim was murdered. Shows the murderer has some skills using a cutting tool when killing the victim".

As detective Jones points to the next officer that put is hand up.

"Do we know what the serrated sharp object is sir?."

Officer Thorton shout out.

"No I haven't got a clue on that. As soon as I know I will inform you all. Is there any more question?."

As the room fell silent for a few minutes.

"That will be all for now your free to go. Just one minute. Anyone get's any new evidence or information in this case report to me. Meeting is now over. Please take the time to look at the board and evidence before going. Also this room will be are new investigation room till the murderer is caught. So next time you come in there be tables to work on and the phone lines are being fitted sometime later on, next week".

As detective Jones picked up the paper from the desk and heads out the door. Followed by detective O' Brien. He makes a call to the morgue. To inform Sophia that both of the detectives were on their way to the morgue and should be around thirty minutes.

Chapter Four

THE AUTOPSY

Sophia went into the cold room with her assistant to prep the victim before the detectives arrived. Where the victim was stored in a box freezer.

The room was a large room kept to the temperature of a fridge with tiles on the floor and white walls. On the right side was a large freezer set on a digital temperature of minus eighteen. That was stainless steel and had twenty-five departments. Which was square and only went a meter across and down. Also the length of a body inside it and contained a stainless steel slab with a cushion pillow for the head to rest on. Attached to rails so the slabs could be pushed in or pulled out. So the body can lay on the slabs and freeze to prevent the bodies from decomposing. For the body's wait for the autopsy to be done. On the left was a large white clock and in the middle of the room was two stainless steel table slabs that contained plug holes at the bottom. For liquid to run down. A jet spray that hung over them, with stainless steel springs around the rubber pipe so you were able to pull down for the water to spray and use between both table slabs. Just between the slabs was a weighing scale that hung from the ceiling with a stainless steel bowl that sat on the scales. Both jet spray and weighing scales hung four foot from the floor. The stainless steel trolley on wheels, which was situated below the weighing scales had utensil laid neatly. Also on the table was a camera. On the ceiling was a microphone which was attached to a metal arm. So that the microphone could be brought down to the level and moved around the area of the table slabs for the person to speak into. The microphone was also connected to a recorder. Which was situated in another part of the building. The recorder was six foot high and three foot across, with a big tape deck the size of a car wheel. So that it could be recorded for hours without being changed. Also connected to the computer so that the recording could be laser burned onto a compact disk.

The assistant was a young man in his early twenties that had spiked black hair with brown eyes and very slim. He was mixed race by having two different race parents. One from tenerife and the other was english. His name was Hugo Fitzgerald and he had his normal clothes underneath his white jacket and white trainers. Hugo Fitzerald went to college one day a week so he could qualify as a coroner. While working as an assistant to help him learn the skills as well as the theory. He was a very quiet person and shy. Always took time before getting used to poeple. Before he was able to talk to people. He had only been in Britain for a year and was very good with his english. As it was a second taught language in their classes as kids. Hugo Fitzerald came from a small island. know as tenerife were he left to better his life.

Sophia and the assistant pulled the slab out with the victim's body laid on it and slid the body across using the white sheet that was wrapped around the victim. Wheeling the bed over to the slabs. Then did the same onto the right slab in the middle of the room. They both carefully took the sheet off by not causing anymore brusing or damage to the victim and left the victim laid on the slab naked with a white sheet placed on top of the victim covering the head to toes and to defrost the victim for the autopsy. That didn't take long as the body was only semi-frozen. While waiting for the detectives to arrive.

The phone rang and Sophia picked up the receiver and pressed it lightly against her ear.

"Hello."

"Hi, Sophia it is detective Jones we on our way shouldn't be too long."

As the voice came across the other side of the receiver.

"Ok, see you in a bit detective Jones."

As Sophia placed the receiver back on the phone. Detective Jones and detective O' Brien stood in the reception waiting for Sophia to come and take them to the cold room. Detective O' Brien stood there reading a magazine that she picked off a pile that was left on the coffee table in the middle of the reception.

The reception room was a small box room that had wooden planks in the colour of pine with certificates in glass frames of qualifications and insurance papers. Six wooden chairs with cushions on the sitting part and a little cushion on the back part of the chair. Dark blue and gold pattern shaped on the cushions of the chair. Three chairs each side against the walls, of the wooden coffee table. Magazine on one and leaflets on the other side of the table. Above the white wooden door with square glass in the top part of the door. That you can only see from the other side of the door was a round clock. On the right side of the door, was an old intercom with a small red button that you press to alert staff. That people are present within the reception area and a camera in a rounded dark coloured plastic case on the ceiling by the entrance door. That was glass with metal stainless steel at the top and bottom on the door. With two key holes and a metal stainless steel in the middle which came out to make a handle on both sides of the door, with a yale keyhole. As the door open Sophia and her assistant stepped out to greet the detectives.

"Hello Sophia this is my partner detective O' Brien."

As Sophia stood looking detective O' Brien up and down. Detective O' Brien put out her hand to shake Sophia hand. while Sophia did the same.

"I would like you to meet my assistant Hugo Fitzgerald. Who will be assisting me while the autopsy takes place."

As both detectives shake the assistants hand. Then passing the shoe box to Sophia that contained the evidence bag. Still keeping the brown envelope with the letter inside the jacket suit pocket. Ready for when Sophia asked for it. All four of them went down the corridor into the cold room where the victim laid underneath the white sheet. Where Sophia and the assistant put on clean plastic gloves and a heavy rubber black apron. Before doing this both of them washed their hands and put black wellies on. Sophia then took out the shoe box and placed the hair and skin above the victim's head onto the slab the victim laid on. Both detective's stood two foot from the slab so they were not in the way and each side of the slab stood Sophia and the assistant. Pulling the sheet off the victim. Sophia checked the victim over before speaking into the microphone. As she pulled the microphone toward her.

"Time eleven thirty-two am, date June 27th 2014. Persons involved with the report are myself, Dr Sophia Portess, my assistant Hugo Fitzgerald, detective Jones and detective O' Brien. Victim Kayleigh Southen, age twenty-six. On the trolley contains a brown paper bag with the victim clothes in for examination of any foreign items that could be found as evidence. Sealed with information of the victim and contents contain in the bag. The victim has bruising marks on her left and right arm a centimetre from the wrist on both arms. Caused by some sort of rope or string tied around them. The same bruising marks are around both ankle areas. Which show that the victim has been tied up on both arms and legs. This indicates the victim had been dead while she was still tied up. Underneath both arms the victim has bruising caused by the way the victim was picked up after the victim had died. Just above the genital part of the area. Up to the belly button has been cut opened. The cut has been straight and looks as if a surgical sharp object has been used and the intestine have been pulled out and tucked back into the stomach area. Leaving the intestine to hang out of the stomach area slightly. This means the murderer has used a surgical knife with a pointed sharp end. So the skin is able to be pierced when cutting into the stomach. Causing the intestine to spill out of the hole that was mayed as the murderer entered the inside of the stomach area".

Sophia moved to the top part and picked up the hair, placing it carefully into the missing part of the head. To see if it fitted before placing it down in the same place she picked it up. Pulling the microphone towards her she starts to speak again.

"The hair and skin have been removed from the crown of the head. Which the skull is showing. A different kind of object has been used in this area. Leaving zig zag in the skin that is left on the head with the remaining hair. Also causing teeth marks from the blade on the skull. By the way the hair and skin have been cut off, has caused the brian fluid to come out of the right ear. This means the murderer was lefthanded. The hair sample that was contained in a plastic bag. Prevented the excess blood from the skin to leak into the cardboard box. This matches the area where the skin and hair used to be. Also causing blood to stain the victim hair turning the blond hair to a red colour. The box is cardboard and has the name that is imprinted onto both sides of the box. This means at some point the box was used as a shoe box. The cardboard box show on one side that the sticker containing a barcode and information on it. Was carefully removed only leaving the glue chemical on the box where the sticker used to be".

Sophie carefully pried open the mouth of the victim breaking the jaw. As she wedged the mouth open by not causing any more damage to the victim's mouth while doing this. Using a swab to run around the edge of the mouth by gathering saliva onto the cotton swab. Placing it into a small plastic see though bag and placing detail of the victim and sample taken onto the bag before putting it onto the trolley. Just below the utensils on the bottom shelf of the trolley. Grabbing the microphone as she speaks into it.

"The mouth has slight bruising around the corners of the lips. Which means some sort of object has been placed into the mouth of the victim. A sample of saliva as been taken from the victim's mouth and sealed for examination for any evidence that might show up. Of the object that was placed into the mouth of the victim".

Sophia picked up the camera. Taking picture of the arms and underneath the arms, legs, stomach and head. Also the hair and skin that had been removed and the shoe box with the plastic bag the hair and skin were in. That was sitting on the trolley placing them onto the table slab on the other side. Taking pictures of them and sealing them up into evidence bags with a label of the victim and contents of the items. Within the evidence bags, placing them back onto the trolley with the saliva sample. The evidence bag containing the clothes. Sophia removed the clothes from the bag and placed then neatly. Laying them out on the table slab on the other side. Taking pictures and then placing the clothes back into the evidence bag sealing it up and putting the bag with the other evidence bags. Getting her assistant to hold open the victim's mouth while Sophia took close up pictures inside the mouth. Using the flash that lit the inside of the mouth as she clicked the button on top of the camera. The assistant then turned the victim's body onto her left side so she could continue. While he held the victim on her side. As Sophia took the microphone around the table slab she began to speak.

"On the back of the Victim we have a reddish mark on both shoulder blades where the victim has pressure sores of grade one and abrasion marks on the both cheeks of the bottom. Caused by the victim being dragged and caused by the gritted. While the murderer dragged the victim's body along the floor. To the point where the murderer wedged the victim against the wall in the alleyway. Also I am able to see grade one pressure sores on both cheeks and heels of both feet. At the back of the feet on the heels. The victim has several abrasion marks where the victim has been dragged along the floor. Also pressure marks on the victim means she had been laid on her back for some time. Areas of the back spine and back of the neck. Where the body had been dead for a while and left in the sitting position for a while. Has cause little pressure mark to run down the back, along the backbone".

Sophia takes some more pictures of the area that had been pointed out and then got the assistant to turn the victim onto her right side. Sophia and the assistant then turned the victim onto her front so she was able to take pictures of the back of the victim. Sophia and the assistant then laid the victim back on her back. She then swabbed the genital area and sealed the swab up into an evidence bag placing it with the others. Sophia then speaks into microphones.

"I have taken all pictures of all the areas containing bruising, pressure sores and the mouth of the victim. I have swabbed the genital area of the victim and sealed the swab into an evidence bag where it will be checked for semen or any other body fluid"

Sophia picks up the drill and places the sharp blade onto the end of it and speaking through the microphone.

"Starting from the head I will cut through the skull to check the brain and weight the brain on the scales."

As Sophia cut around the head of the victim with the drill. Taking fifteen minutes she carefully separated the skull from the top of the head. She then picked up the shape small knife and cut around the edges of the skull, to release the brain. While doing this, the assistant used the surgical spirit. Then placed the brain onto the scales and recorded the weight. Speaking into the microphone. As she was picking up the next surgical tools Sophia needed.

"The Weight of the brain is normal, no concern. Next I will weight the lungs and the heart".

Sophia cut from the bottom of the neck to the top of the stomach. Picking up the item to hold the skin back as she drills down the centre of the rib cage. Lifting the ribs up and removing the lungs carefully with the surgical knife and weighted the lungs. Then removed the heart and weighted it. Placing the lungs and heart back into the same place she had removed them from.

"The weight of the lungs is normal. Also the discoloured lungs means the victim was a smoker. The weight of the heart is normal. I will now weight the liver".

As Sophia opened the area of the stomach and weighted the organ, speaking into the microphone. slowly going through the stomach area. She noticed something wrong that didn't show up in her medical report. Which she picked up for from the G.P. on the way back from the station. Carrying on speaking through the microphone.

"It appears the victim's womb has been removed. By taking into count that medical records. The victim has no surgery, that states the womb being removed. On the victim's medical history and the way it had been cut out. The womb was removed by an amateur. This caused the victim's pressure to rise. Making the victim's pain unbearable. As the person cut into the flesh of the victim. While keeping the victim alive when removing the womb. This made her go into a state of shock causing the body to bleed out at a rapid rate as the murderer punctured several arteries. Therefore I am diagnosing the death of the victim from loss of blood causing the victim to go into shock causing cardiac arrhythmia attack. End of report, time twelve fifty two pm".

Sophia walks into a different room. Returning with a form she had to fill in and handed it to detective Jones. The form had information of the autopsy on it. With a reference number given for the autopsy. So that if the police needed any information for the autopsy that was just completed. By given the reference number it would be easy to retrieve the information as it would be logged and saved on the computer. Even though the reports were filed it was faster to find them on the computer.

"A copy of the full report will be with you in the next four hours and I will drop it off personally at the office at five pm".

After the detective's had gone. Sophia then went back to sort out the victim with her assistant. That was still laid on the slab with her stomach still open. Sophia and her assistant finished sewing the victim up before placing the victim back into the freezer. As the detective's arrived back at the station. Detective Jones sat in his office taking a few second before picking up the receiver. While detective 'O' Brien went to the canteen to get drinks for her and detective Jones.

Detective Jones found himself in a situation when going after the scalp slayer murderer. When the true unfolds itself. Something that happen in his passed life revealing the truth. A game played with clue's given. Detective Jones must work the clues out to find the next victim before the murderer get there first. Will he stop the murderer in their tracks. By winning the game will be the only way to stop any more murders from happening.

Chapter Five

THE NEWS

"This is the six O' clock news by Kemp Norman and Susan Blates. The main story is a young woman named. Kayleigh Southen, age 26 years old. Been found early hour's this morning. By the Freeman Street Market, murdered. A police report will be given tonight at the town hall on the information the police have so far. We go live to the town hall where Mr Patten is at this moment. Mr Patten, what do you have so far on the murdered victim?".

Kemp Norman was a middle-aged man in a brown suit with a white check shirt and brown tie. He had blue eyes with short dark hair. While sat behind a long rounded desk, holding paper's in his hands has he read out the news.

"Well I spoke to the chief inspector Karl early today and as far as we know it is a young girl that was murder and her body was found at one thirty a.m. this morning. At this time we don't know when she had been murdered or how she was murdered?. They have no leads at this present time and will not be given any information out at this time on the investigation. Till tonight when they hold the press meeting. All I know is that the chief inspector Karl, detective's Jones and detective O' Brien are dealing with the investigation and all chief inspector Karl as released so far is the young women name. Kayleigh Southen and age twenty-six years old. Who has been murdered and the family of the young woman, have been informed. Which the police will not be given out any information on the family whereabouts. Due to grieving and the family requested to be kept out of publicity. They are going to release all other information at the town hall tonight on how she was murdered and the evidence they have so far on the case. The madam chief commissioner, Miss Wright who run Yorkshire and Lincolnshire areas on crime. Will be at the town hall attending the press meeting. Also on this issue there will be a reading of the report they got back from Dr Portess early today. After an autopsy was carried out on the young woman in question. Where they will be given the outcome on what they know so far on the autopsy reporter and some evidence that showed up later in the day. Which chief inspector Karl said "This evidence that was received by detective Jones could be the key answer to solving the case and bring the murderer to justice". This is all I know at the present time. I am able to get back to you when I get more of an update on this, on the ten O' clock news".

Mr Patten was a tall slim man stood on the opposite side of the road holding a microphone in his left hand with a blue suit and tie that had gold pattern in. He was fair skin with light blond hair and blue eyes. As he stood in front of the camera. You were able to see the town hall behind him from the other side of the road.

As the screen went blank. While detective Jones stood with his fingertip pressed firmly on the off button, on the tv control. Has he pointed the tv control at the tv that was sat on the wall in one of the training rooms at the police station. Stood next to him was the madam chief commissioner, chief inspector and detective O' Brien. He laids the tv control onto the desk and picked up the autopsy report, that he received from Sophia an hour ago. Turning to his work colleagues. He gave them the nod, to indicate he was ready to leave for the press meeting at the town hall.

The room was a size of a football pitch with an old fashion carpet and wall's that had red at the bottom and cream at the top. Golden dado rail that separated the two colours on the walls. On top of the ceiling was two big size crystal chandeliers that hung down and lite up the room. At the back of the room was refreshment that sat on a long table with a red tablecloth. Cups and saucers with a large hot water boiler. For making drinks with and a lite snack. On each side of the room was three camera's that stood six foot high. Positioned on a turntable, so the cameras were able to move around in all direction when filming the press meeting. Control by a camera person for each camera in the room and each camera person had a headphone on with a small microphone that stuck out from the side of the headphone. In front of the camera person mouth. Just in the top right corner of the room was a number of monitors. Sat just above a control panel with a number of control switches. By controlling all six camera's and the sound and base when filming the press meeting. It was linked to the main headquarter's of the news studio. Showing what was being film though all six cameras on each monitor and the main monitor that was to give the final result for broadcasting the press meeting. Before it was shown on tv. Run by two people who both had the same head phone's on, as the camera people. So that they were able to communicate with all six camera's people. By telling them when to zoom in or zoom out and the direction they wanted the camera's to film, at the present time. In the centre of the room was around hundred gold plated chairs with material that was the same red colour as the walls. That covered the seated part and the back part of the chairs. The reporter sat on the chair with some of them having camera's around their necks and other's sat with their notebook and cheap biro's as they wrote down the information given from the meeting. On the right side was six big windows that went two inches from the floor and ten inches from the top of the ceiling. That had been covered by wooden window shutters, to block the day light out. By preventing the sunlight from blinding the camera's, as they film the press meeting. Sat at the front of the room on a big long table with three microphones that stuck up and three glasses of water for each person. Sitting at the table was the madam chief commissioner in the centre. To the left was the chief inspector and to the right was detective Jones. Just on the left of the door was detective O'Brien who stood there watching as the press meeting began. On each side of the long table was two women sitting in front of a typewriter, typing in shorthand. Everything that was said within the press meeting. Which was then logged on to the report when back at the police station.

One lady was a oldies woman with grey curly hair. Containing purple highlights around the top of her hair. She was short and chubby with a silky white dress with blue flowers as the pattern. Wearing glasses with purple rim's, that covered her face. Also she had her thumb missing of her right hand, due to an accident she had a year prior.

The other lady was an Afican woman with dark curly hair. Plated back to give a neat finish. She was middle age and very slim body with chubby cheeks. Wearing an African dress with an African head piece that covered the head. The jewellery that she was wearing was big bracelets and big earrings that dangle down. Made out of some bamboo stick with eccentric colourful patterns.

As the lights from the camera flickered within the room and the clicking sound as the Madam chief commissioner spoke into the microphone.

"Good evening to you all. Before I start, I like to say a few things. I am madam chief commissioner, Miss Mandi Wright who deals with crime over the Yorkshire and Lincolnshire areas. To my left is chief inspector, Mr Karl Johnson Who runs the Grimsby and Cleethorpes police station and to my right is detective, Mr Chris Jones who is in charge of this case at the Grimsby police station. Not forgetting, just in the corner by the door is detective, Miss Jessica O' Brien, who is detective Jones partner on this case. For any future references regarding this case. These will be the officers you need to speak to. Including myself, if you need to ask any question on the case. We will also be release anymore information regarding the case as and when new evident's reveal itself."

The madam chief commissioner grabs hold of the glass of water and took a sip. Placing the glass back onto the surface of the table. Before speaking again.

The madam chief commissioner was a middle age woman with blue eyes and rosy white cheeks. The hair was blond tied back into a ponytail. With makeup literally put on and red lipstick that made her lips look healthy. Wearing a dark blue suit with a purple blouse, were the collier folded over the jacket of the suit. She spoke in a mature and firm way. Who was a boss that got results within the Yorkshire and Lincolnshire area's when dealing with crime. Has she was the type of woman that loved her job and dedicated her life to perform high results. The madam chief commissioner also was annotated for rewards. Over the past couple of year for lowering the crime in the areas of Yorkshire and Lincolnshire. She had been published by the top high street magazine for achieving the best results and receiving the rewards.

"Early hours this morning at one thirty a.m. detective Jones arrived at Freeman Street Market, where a young lady was discovered in a sitting up position. The hair and skin from the top of her head had been removed. The young lady was pronounced dead on arrival. We can confirm that the victims was Miss Kayleigh Southan, age twenty six year old and she had been murdered. At this time we have very few leads to the person who had murdered Miss Kayleigh Southan or any murderer weapons that was used to take this young girl's life from her. We do have one of the leads that detective Jones discovered at nine forty-five a.m. today. When receiving a shoe box that contained, the hair and skin. Which was confirmed that it matches the hair and skin of Miss Kayleigh Southan. With a letter addressed to detective Jones by the murderer. I will now put you over to detective Jones who will read the letter that he received."

"Good evening I just like to say that the letter did knock me back abit when I read it as the murderer seems to know me and being watching me as I dealt with the case. The letter reads:

Hello detective Jones or shall I just call you Chris,
Yes I will call you by your first name I hope you were inspired by the artwork I left for you to find, no not right. had to deal with, much better may I say. Hope that you didn't get

too wet this morning. Especially when taking time to have a smoke. But I believe I had the best view ever. Watching you do your work not forgetting to clean away my art. Yes it was most beautiful work I ever did especially while listening to the most relaxing music. It didn't help that she had to scream while being tied up and had to have her mouth stuff with a cloth. It ruined the music abit. But I can say the feeling I got looking into her scared eyes before they went as cold as ice. Was like the best thrill I got in my life I can say it was better, much better than sex. well getting back to business, as I don't want to let you know all my dirty secrets now or do I. Oh by the way I thought you could do with that hair I sent you, so you can cover that patch on your head and maybe you can take that hat off you wear. Because I must say it doesn't suit you that much, only joking!. It a trophy for you, so that everyone know of my beautiful artwork.

As you can see the murderer has been watching every move on the case. He/She could be sat in here with us at this very moment. The Letter go on by given us certain clues:

As I sit there my kids sleeping in bed, watching the soaps. This is the end that has come for me, as I see my life passing away. First the fear, then the rope marks Following with a sharp pain. Now it is time to close my eyes and as I walk though as a spirit in time. I'll watch as my kids get a pleasant surprise. When they awaken to find their single mum passed away on the carpeted floor, with the tv still playing to itself. you have two days to find where I live. One adult, two kids in a house that's opposite a roundabout somewhere near Grimsby but not far from town. Maybe Cleethorpe or maybe not and has three rooms to sleep in. so tick, tick and tick the clock strikes again?.

The clues we have are, the murderer will strike again and he/she has given use forty-eight hours. We are in the present of tracking down the woman and two children. Living in a three bedroom house. Across Grimsby and Cleethorpes area's nears all roundabouts within the next thirty-six hours that we have left. The letter goes on to say:

So there you go the clue has started to go. Will you make it or will you not make it and let her go. two days you have no more, no less. So work it out or not as she has less than a couple of days to live or die. You only can be the one who decides her fate. As dinner approaches. I hunger for the meat she contains near her stomach, down below I cut the meat out and fry meat for my lunch. Taste of the meat will give me that taste for more. So who am I?.

This means we are not dealing with just a serial killer. We are also dealing with a cannibal who eats human body parts. At the end of the letter the murderer has given name that they wish to be call:

P.S. my name is an old indian story, not too look too far as the hair will give you the clue to my name and I will be known for years as the killer who made the 10 'o' clock news. While making my art go on and on.

The old indian story is that the indian believed that if they took the skin and hair of there enemies. They wouldn't be able to be pulled to heaven. We have now decided to name the murderer the scalp slayer and the case is known as the scalp slayer murders referances number case 247. I will now pass you back to the madam cheif commissioner Miss Wright".

As detective Jones laid down the letter in front of him still sealed in the see though evident bag. As he cringed his eyes slightly from the flashing lights of the cameras.

"I like to say that we have officers working around the clock to find this address and to being the murderer to justices. An autopsy has been done and an report on how Kayleigh Southan died. I will pass you onto the chief inspector Karl who will read the report out given by Dr Portess at five p.m. today"

"Good evening to you all. I just like to say that I send my condolences out to the family for their loss of their loved one. At five p.m. today we received a report on the autopsy of Kayleigh Southan. That took place at eleven thirty-two a.m. With the present of Dr Portess, her assistant, detective Jones and detective O'Brien. The report says:

The deceased was Kayleigh Southan, aged twenty-six. Died at approximately twelve hours from the time the autopsy took place. Making time of death at eleven thirty p.m. The Autopsy revealed that the victim hair and skin had been removed from the crown of the head. That the hair and skin that was identified by detective Jones from a shoe box was addressed to detective Jones. Matched the skin and hair of the victim's head. That a jagged object was used. Causing the zig zags into the skin and has the murderer carved into the skin. Making the victim brain fluid to leak out of the right ear. At this moment the item used, as not been identified at the present time. The autopsy also revealed the victim had an organ removed from the belly button to bottom of the stomach. That show the victim's womb had been removed. Checking the victim medical record show that the victim had not been for any major operation. Involving the womb being removed. The same sort of object used on the hair and skin. Was not used when taken the womb, it was a different kind of object that was used like a surgical knife. Causing the victim to go into cardiac arrhythmia attack. That has been diagnosed as the cause of death. Where several arteries were punctured. Making the victim body bleed rapid. So the victim died of lose of blood. During the autopsy a number of abrasions and brusing on the victim body was found. Around the body. The victim had brusing to the mouth where some sort of item was wedged into the mouth. Around the legs and wrest by some item tired, to prevent the victim. From able to move during the procedure. Making the victim still alive when he cut into the stomach as the murderer removed the organ in question. The abration that accrued from bottom, heels and back was that the victim had been moved at the time of death. By dragging the victim body along the floor and the first-degree presure sore was from where the body had been in one place for an number of hours".

Has inspector karl removed his reading glasses. Rubbing his eyes. While placing his glasses gengle down onto the table next to the glass of water, before he spoke again.

"just a couple of things I like to add is that we believe that the murderer is left hand. From the way he cut into the skin at the crown of the head which was the reason for the brain fluid to drained out off the right ear. The other is that the murderer is an amateur and could be learning from a book or have a profession in cooking has it states the murderer likes to eat human organs. Maybe the murderer could be suffering from mental health. I now pass you back to the madam chief commissioner Miss Wright"

"I Just like to say is that we are working around the clock to solve the case and bring the murderer to justices. I have a number of offices including detective Jones and detective 'O' Brien. By tracking down the next victim before the murderer kills again. So just like to say that if there any woman out there living on their own with two children. To contact the number on the screen as it could save your life. Also if anyone see or hear anything please contract us on the number as if we all work together. We be able to stop the murderer."

As the commissioner finished what she was saying, all three of them stood up and headed out the door. With the camera still rolling and flashing light from the cameras still going while they leave the room.

Chapter Six

THE NEW RECRUITS

"Right what do we have so far boys and girls. I need to hear results, we only have less than twenty-four hours left."

As detective Jones swung open the door, with a banging noise as the edge of the door handle made contacted with the wall. Detective 'O' Brien walks toward detective Jones holding a Bundle of white sheets of papers that were clipped together and tucked between a brown paper back folder in her hand. Resting against her hip has she walked towards detective Jones.

"We have so far information on single mums within Grimsby and Cleethorpes areas. A list of just under a thousand. Which was received a few hours ago by fax from the council. Who listed all names and addresses. That we are sorting through at this present time and listing all single mums who live near a roundabout's in Grimsby and Cleethorpes areas, with two kids. All item found at the scene has been dusted for fingerprints and some of the items dusted haven't showed any fingerprints. Of the victim but the items that did not come up with fingerprints had been wiped clean. The clothing from the victim has no DNA on it. But the report did say that there were powder substances found on the clothing that matches the same powder substance from a latex disposable gloves. Which means that the murderer was using disposable gloves. Which I sent a couple of offices back to the crime scene area and up to a three-mile radius from the crime scene to recheck the crime area. Bins and alleyways where the murderer might had disposed the gloves when leaving the crime scene. I now put all pictures and pinned up all evidence taken from the scene onto the board. Using a black marker pen. I wrote down just below them. The item's found, numbers given by the forensics and location of the area. Where the item's had been photographed or bagged as evidence. Also all cameras have been checked and vehicles seen within the area of the crime scene. Around two hours before the victim was found, up to the time the victim was found. By checking the number plates of every vehicle through our database. Revealing the owners name and address of every vehicle identified within that time frame. At this present time the two officers are interview all owners of vehicles identified at their home. Officers that interviewed people around the area and the people who were stood around watching. Have come back. The persons questioned by are offiers had all said. That they had not seen anything or heard anything during the time before and up to the victim was found. There was one thing that show on the list of single mum's with two kids, Sophia. She matches the criteria. Shown up within the letter. So I have organised an patrol to watch over Sophia house. as she a single mum with two children living in Cleethorpes by a roundabout."

While detective 'O' Brien handed detective Jones the folder containing copies of the fax sent. Listing all the information of single mum's within the Grimsby and Cleethorpes areas. With names and address found so far. That had been circled in red highlighter of mum's with two children living next to a roundabout.

"Does she know."

As a nerve feeling creed over detective Jones body. That made him feel anxious. Knowing the information. Of a close lover was at risk of danger.

"No, I thought that we should keep this one out of the loop from Sophia. It might panic her. Which could mess up the investigation and she not clicked on yet. From when she examine the letter."

While she Stood there worrying. If she did the right thing not letting Sophia know that she was one of the people on the list.

"Good, you did right. So don't look so worried ok. I would have done the same thing and kept Sophia out of the loop. As I know that she be ok with officers keeping an eye on her without her knowing. Maybe your right on the ball mark. As the murderer know me and might target the one, I am close too."

As he stood there. Putting on a brave face. While sweating from the palms of his hands as he thinks of Sophia. At this point detective Jones walk over and stands to look at the whiteboard that was fill with evidence of the case. While gently rubbing his top lip with his index finger. That also rubbed across the nose as he stood thinking about the next move of the murderer. At this point the chief inspector Karl walked into the room with a group of people unknown to the station. Where detective Jones was standing. As he spoke out it made detective Jones jerk suddenly. While he was trance figuring out the case from the evidence he had.

"Detective Jones I like you to meet some people from M.I.5. headquarters."

As detective Jones turned around and glanced at the unknown people. Stood next to the chief inspector Karl. Turning his sight back to the chief inspector Karl. While listening to what was being said.

"The first person I like you to meet is professor Willincole. Who work for M.I.5. Also part time teacher at Cambridge University that teaches classes on how a murderer mind work."

Professor Willincole was a oldies guy with dark greyish hair. That was cut short and comb to one side. He had brown eyes and thick bushy eyebrows. A nose that contained an oversize bridge causing the nose to point downward more at the end of his nose. His face was chubby as the cheek bones were hidden. Given him a double chin and hardly any neck. His lips were thin and he was very clean shaven. He spoke in a low tone. By making you very calm and at ease. The man was slightly over average weight and is belly hanged over his trouser. Hidden by the jumper. He had checked light brown shirt on. That you notice from the collier, folded over the neck part of the jumper. With the top button loosens, leaving a gap. The darkish brown pattern jumper. Made from wool and looked old and tacky. On his right arm where the jumper sleeve. Was slightly pushed up is arms. revealing the thick heavy silver watch. Chipped just above his hand. Containing lots of little silver metal bars, clipped together to make the strap of the watch and a square piece that clipped over to hold the watch in place. You could notice the hair from his arm. Where poking through the gaps between the little silver metal bars of the straps. His trousers were dark brown that had the centre line iron into the trousers which showed an out print off a leather belt from the jumper. That hid his belly which was hanging over his trousers. With black slip-on shoes, giving off a dull shine to them.

"Hi it nice to meet you detective Jones. I am here to understand the murderer by acknowledging the way the murderer thinks and acts when abducting a victim. Upon the time of murdering the victim and the murderer signature. As every murderer will murder by leaving their mark so that they show a personal degree and stamp that they muedered the victim. Where all murderer believe in signing their work, like an artists. By understanding the way the murderer feels inside. How the murderer pick the victim. The upbringing of the murderer life and the point that cause the murderer to start murdering the victims. In most cases it usually when a person has been a victim their self or they do petty crimes, injured or kill aminals to start off and maybe change the crime which ends up where the person would more likely be sentenced for stealing, sex offences and violence. Before they progress to the next stage. Where the murderer will more likely make mistakes at first and learns to get better at times by leaving fewer evidence of them being there".

While detective Jones may his acquaintance with professor Willincole. The chief inspector Karl started to speak.

"The second person is Dr Harpe that works also at M.I.5.. That train in graphologist and is able to tell you about a person by their handwriting."

Dr Harpe was a thin and very tall man. That had curly light brown hair which hung down just passed his ear. Covering most of the ears. Only revealing the top part of his ears. He had blue eyes with long eyelashes and eyebrows that were thin. Making the eye browe hard to see as they camouflage with the colour of the skin. The nose that dip down the middle of his face was long and pointed at the tip of the nose. With oversize nostrils. Causing them to spread out. As the outer part of the nostrils wedges against the puffy reddish cheeks. His chin was stuck out slightly. Which contained dimple in the centre and a smallish mouth. Which only showed the tonge, has Dr Harpe pressed his lips against his teeth. That over laped the top of his teeth, while he spoke. The adams apple stuck out, resting in the middle of the skinny neck. All you could do was frocus on the adams apple that moved up and down. While Dr Harpe talked very fast with an IQ higher than aveage. Making others puzzed while they listen to what was being said. He used words that were long, not used as offend and used more in professional medical terms. That mayed people, confused and not able to understand. While their mouths dropped open. Staring at him, unable to take hardly any information into their brains and frowning their eye from what Dr Harpe was saying. He had a red shirt with a black tie. The shirt was unbuttoned at the top between the collier and the tie was slightly hanging down in a loop from the collier. Disappearing around the neck as the collier folded over. The gap where the shirt parted open, showed abit of Dr Harpe chest. Was tips of the chest hair. That rested onto the shirt as it cuvred over. The shirt was tucked into his black trousers. With a lether black belt, that contained a faded goldish buckle. Which had been pulled tight around his waist. Causing the shirt to creased around the edges of the belt. This put pressure on his skin and hips. Making him walk like he had messed himself. This made others in the room. Think he was batting for the othe side. Even know he was straight as can be and never slepted with a guy in his life. His trousers were creased sharply and neatly down the middle with an iron. Leaving a slightly smooth shiny mark around the edges of the creased trousers. As the iron burned the creases as he pressed hard onto the trousers. While running the iron down the folded trousers to make a straight sharp crease line onto the front and back of the trousers.

His shoes were black, that had pattens around the front edges and the laces where neatly tired into a bow. Tucked underneath the bottom of his trousers. Showing the dark blue sports socks, between the gaps of the trousers and shoes.

"It an acquaintance to meet you detective Jones. I've been so looking forward to using my ability of graphologist to overcome the obstacles that you have specified, with great passion. Putting the mind into balance and becoming one with the letter. Semantic Value of each word will give a definition of profiling. Organising and construct. Becoming the subject in question through the contents. Within the section of wording that creates a relationship. Building a knowledge and understanding between me and the murderer. Till a climax becomes a volcano which will expose. Feel and excurse the murderers thoughts into my cortex tissue. Motivating my impulses and processing the supreme brain. So that I can translate the thoughts and wisdom. Crashing system automatic style and revealing the wording between the lines. being the person to distinguished. Taken away satisfaction that they feel and retaining the fulfillment. Before the murderer climax into ejaculation from a chemical reaction that trigger within the brain. Prevent the murderer making a vulnerable person. becoming the next meals. Understanding the letter I am able to over mind the murderer thoughts. Draining the murderer cortex of every energy particles within the murderer brian. Reducing the murderer brain to a peanut with nothing to become but a bag of nerves. leaving no ability to frighten or murderer again. When I catch and look the murderer in the eyes. Pushing the murderer head into the vehicle that will being the murderer to justices and free the world from danger once again".

A silence was broken ten seconds later as detective Jones spoke out. With everyone in the room stopped what they were doing. Stood staring into the direction. Where detective Jones was meeting others.

"I don't know who more sick, you or the murderer as all I hear was something about climax, ejaculation and wanting to be come one with the letter. Well as soon as we catch the murderer I personally give you the letter and you can ejaculate as much as you like".

"In a figure of speech. I was using the wording as a distinctive ways of explaining the outcome of profiling the terms of the letter. Using the knowledge and skills to identify the way the murderer would think, feel and crave. During the planning, time and finishing of every victim the murderer murders."

As Dr Harpe finished speaking the chief inspector Karl spoke out.

"Now that enough from you detective Jones. It totally out of order and disrespectful as you may be in charge of the investigation and these men from M.I.5. Are your supreme officers. That means they are higher rank than you are. So you have no right to be sarcastic and rude toward any of them, do you understand."

At this point professor Willincole spoke out. As detective Jones blushed while a feeling of awkward and speechless.

"I just like to say my partner will use words that are unusual and people will mislead way meaning to what he is saying. But he good at his job and we here to help you bring the murderer in before the murderer strike again. The reason we been call in, is we had a call from the madam chief commissioner at Scotland Yard. She would like to get the situation solved as quickly without any more murders happening. By keeping crime down to a minimum in the Lincolnshire and Yorkshire areas. So we are not here to step on your toes or take over the investigation. Just to use are knowledge and skill to help you with the investigation by stopping the murderer in their tracks as quickly and effectively."

Detective Jones apologized to Dr Harpe for the action he had said.

"I just like to say sorry, for my action and hope I didn't insult you in any way. But it the way you came out with it. Just that you speak fast. Which meant that I only understood certain words. Making it sound sick in the head, from the words I picked up".

As detective Jones held his hands out, shaking Dr Harpes hand. With a reply back from Dr Harpe.

"It very understandable that you would indeterminate. What was said. As this is a comment in alot of people where their mind will side track or a person is unable to process all information taken into the mind. Making the person assumed that they heard something that was totally different. In medical terms this would be the temporal lobe part of the brain. called the primary auditory cortex. Part of the brain that listens to what been said. Processing the information and informing your mind of the information you have listened too. Sometimes by not listen to every word spoken or missing certain words will make the person think something totally different to what has been said. Where in your case you only listened to specific words and by putting two and two together. Coming out with a sum of five. That why you assumed I was pleasuring myself. Over the letter that I will be studying. Which informal terms. I was using the sexual words as profiling. How the murderer would feel inside. Before murdering a victim to the point of disposing of the corpses."

As the chief inspector Karl thanks Dr Harpe for what was said. carried on speaking.

"Just want you to meet one person she not from M.I.5. She a good friend of the family and may help use with the investigation. By using her psychic mind. I like to to meet Kelly-Marie Ramsden".

As the chief inspector Karl spoke out, a young women holding a white stick stood. Holding onto the chief inspector Karl's arm.

Kelly had dark straight hair. That came down past her shoulder. Rosy reddish cheeks, puffed out more when she smile. Her eye brows were kept neatly shaped. Which curved around the top of her eye lids. She had whitish grey eye. Where Kelly went blind from a very young age. You could still see the hazel brown iris in her eyes. Fading away slowly as the years pass by and her pupils had shrunk into pinprick. The nose was small and straight. With dimples separating the cheeks. The corners of her thin reddish lips touch the bottoms of each cheek with her perfect white teeth. That gave a warm hearted smile and a rounded chin. Given her a dimple just below the bottom lip. Kelly was medium build woman, wearing a colourful blouse top with no sleeves and the neckline dip down. Showing part of the chest. A Gold thin necklace with a gold locket. That had tiny diamonds around the edges. Where the locket opens, on either sides and pictures of her love ones sealed inside the locket. The fake bracelets that was rested on her wrists, just above the hands. Where made from different materials. With each one having it own shade of colour. She had a gold ring, containing her birthstone. That sparkled in different segments of the stone. As the light beamed down and reflected the shapes of each segment. The ring was placed on the middle index finger. On her right hand. Her fingernails that been varnish white with glitter. With colourful butterflies. Each butterfly was painted different in the centre with the wings spread out. That covered two-thirds of each nail. As Kelly would spend hours getting her nails done, at the nail shop in town. She had black leggings and leather black boots. Containing at the top of the boots. Was thick white fur with a hint of black added into the colour. Pulling the boots over the bottoms of the legging.

She slowly moved toward detective Jones with the chief inspector Karl, guiding her. Along the way. Using the palms of her hands, placing them onto each side of detective Jones face. To get the feel and shape. While putting an image into her mind of a person she had just met. Hanging around the wrist of her left hand was a velvet white string attached to the stick she used for getting around with. To free her hands while she, became acquainted with detective Jones. She moved her hands around the face. Making sure she didn't miss any part, shape and features that distinguish the appearance of detective Jones. Slowly placing her arms down by her side and stepping back, before speaking.

"Hi detective Jones you're a strange one, just like to say. The feeling I get from you is that you are a very stubborn person. Who will try and get what you want. I feel that there's someone in your life that love's you. But you only care for her and there no love within your heart. I believe this person name begins with the letter S, mmm let think. Ho yes something along the lines of Sophia as the first name. One last thing I see a dark mist around you. But can't quite put my finger on it at this moment of time".

"Ho your good, unbelievable good and that scares me. I must say you have me to a tee. Let just hope with them skill you be able to lead us to the murderer".

As a dribble of sweat down the side of detective Jones face, with him feeling very nervous from the reading Kelly gave him. Then he told her what he thought.

Chapter Seven

RUNNING OUT OF TIME

"Right everyone, I like you all to stop what you doing for a moment. I have a couple of things to say. First one is I would like you all to get to know these new team members. From M.I.5 we have Professor Willincole and Dr Harpe, these are your supreme officers. So you will address, them as sir. The M.I.5 was called in by Scotland Yard. As they feel that it will help us with the case. I will still be in charge and running things around here. They are here to work with me and even know I am in charge. Professor Willincole and Dr Harpe are higher rank officers so they are your bosses and you will do what they ask and respect them. Also have a young lady who is blind so will need help. Till she gets to know the surrounding. Her name is Kelly-Marie Ramdsen, who would like to be called by her first name Kelly. She's a personal friend of chief inspector Karl. Who come in to help with the case as a psychic. Kelly is good at what she does. I was given the experience just a few moments ago. Now, I am very sceptical about people who have psychic powers. By thinking that it was a load of rubbish. But I must say, after hearing what Kelly told me as change my whole aspect of the way I thinking. Well I was shocked by what she told me. As everything that was said is unbelievably spot on. I don't personally know the woman. Never met her before in my life. Just met her and she read me to a tee.

Like she known me for years. The second thing I like to talk about is the time we have left. That it now nearly ten and we have until to night to find the mother of two. I will be busy for a couple of hours. Going through the case with Professor Willincole and Dr Harpe. By bringing them up to date with everything we know and evidence we have so far. So I leave Kelly in your capable hands. Please take good care of her and get her to touch some of the evidence. Which might give her psychic vision of any evidence that we missed and could be a key evidence that leads us to the murderer. I think the murderer letter would be a very good point to start with. I be holding an up to date meeting at sixteen hundred hours. For anyone who not sure that four P.M. So if your taken breaks, make sure that you are all in this room five minutes before or otherwise. I will personally hand out warnings. Now I don't like to be strict. It make me feel bad. But we on a deadline here we no time to lose. That all, I leave you to get on with it. Detective 'O' Brien I will leave in charge while I am out. She help with any question or need to know basis. Anything that comes to light bring it to my attention. I'll be in my office. If I am out for any reason. Pass the message on to detective 'O' Brien and she will ring me on my moblie to imform me of any changes or updates within the case".

When detective Jones finished speaking. Professor Willincole and Dr Harpe made their greeting with the rest of team. Before following detective Jones to his offices. Sitting down in front of his desk while detective Jones pulled his report out of the cabinet. He handed the report file over to the M.I.5 offices and sat in his leather chair. Rocking it slightly back and forward, as he watch them read through the report. As the report was placed onto the desk Professor Willincole spoke out.

"Very interesting, I believe. I seen this kind of behaviour before. This person is very good at what they do. By planning and gathering the information of the victim. Before murdering them. Obviously the murderer as been watching every move you make. You may even meet, seen or know the murderer. With the autopsy report. The victim's womb has been removed and the victim hair was removed. It said in the report that the hair was sent to you in a shoe box. With a letter from the murderer explaining that they were eating a human organ. From the victim that had been removed. This makes me believe that the murderer may have enjoyment eating the human organ and may have issues. I mean by issue. That a woman needs a womb to have babies and that could be a key point. The murderer could have lost a child or they are infertile. Making the murderer unable to have a children or bear a child. The hair that was sent to you is a sign that the murderer is signing the work. Just to let you know that the murder victim was one of the murderer's. Given the murderer satisfaction that everyone knows. The victim was one of the murderer's and making the murderer feel they are becoming famous. Which the murderer feels, that the victim is their master peace. Known as their artwork. This is why the murderer has sent you part of the victim. As a signature of there art peace. It also says in the report, the letter informed you. The murderer wanted to be named. I believe the name the murderer wanted, stated an old indian story. About removing the hair to prevent the spirit, going to heaven. In theory the murderer already knew that you would name them. The scalp slayer by given you the indian story. That why the indian story was used within the letter. That means the murderer must attend church every Sunday and believe that the victims sinned. So the murderer takes the hair off the victims. To prevent the spirit entering heaven. This gives me an indication that the murderer is very well educated. It states that part of the letter was written in a riddle. Given clues of the next victim. Now why would the murder do this, let me think. Yes, by given a clue to the next victim. Is not to be caught. No, very smart move. The murderer is playing a game of chess. I mean, think of a chess board. Each piece and a game of chess. Now think how the chess pieces are laid out, what each piece does and how you would play the game. In a game of chess. You have to think eight steps ahead and the next eight move the other player will play. This is exactly what we have, a game of chess. Where every games is a victim's life and every victim we don't save in time. Means the murderer has won and will start a new game. By the murderer selecting the next victim. The murderer sent you clues in a riddle. This means you are automatically playing the game. So to solve the riddle. We have to think like chess and play the next eight move. The only way to make the moves is by working out the next move the murderer will make. Revealing the answers to the clues and check mate the murderer. By given the murderer no more moves. Is the only way we will win this game. Eight moves mmm, got it the moves are. The victim, the children, the house, the location, roundabout, time, date and the room. These are the eight moves that we have to think about. Which will hold the key to the answers, to the clues. Let see!, the victim. We know she a single mother of two. So it as to be a woman between early twenties, up to late forties. The reason for this, most woman will stop having their period in their late fourties. Which means they no longer be able to have children. The murderer wants a woman who can have children. giving the person pleasure when they take away the victim's motherhood. The children!, my understanding is that the children are sleeping in bed at the time the victim is murder. Also states the children will get a pleasant surprise when they wake up. Indicating the children will be the ages around toddler to nine maybe ten years old. Due to the time the children are in bed. The house!, what type of house?. I would say we looking for a three bedrooms house with front and back garden. The front garden would probably have a bin filled up and rubbish bags that are placed beside the bin. Resting against the wall of the house. With a stone path. There probably be cracks in the path and weeds growing through. The grass area will likely have patches in and there be flower scattered over the grass area. At the back you more likely see an open space, with a shed. There be toys, bikes and a padding pool that been fill with sand and plastic coloured ball. Location! we know it is in Grimsby or Cleethorpes area. Roundabout! which means the house is more likely be a corner house on a busy road. Making it hard for other residents in the area. To hear any noises when the murderer is taking the victim life. Time! when the soaps are on. This means the murderer will strike between the hours of six p.m. and nine p.m. Very smart move, according to research a higher percentage of people watch television when soaps are on. This means that it be less likely anybody. Will see or hear anything. The date! The murderer wrote in the letter. I give you two days. It also say's in the letter. No more or no less. Then it say that she as less than two days. That puzzle's me, why would the murderer murder the victim earlier. If the letter was written after you found the body?. That's something I have to work out later. It might be a key answer. Last of all, the pattern the murderer users. The victims are young to mid-age women. The murderer removes the womb and eats womb. Slicing the victims hair and sending the hair as a signature. The murderer plans every murder, writing a letter with a riddle. Address personally to you and listen to music, while murdering the victims. These are all a pattern that the murderer using. Which identifies the kind of murderer we are looking for."

While detective Jones sat with his back resting against the back of the leather chair, clenching his index fingers tightly around the front of the chair arms. As he listens to Professor's Willincole feedback from the report he had just looked through. Turning his head slightly, as Dr Harpe gave his feedback.

"My understanding of the murderer is. From a young age the murderer was brought up in a middle-classed family. Went to boarding school during the week and at weekend. Holidays and half terms. The murderer would spend time with their family. Probably the murderer would injure animals or killed them. The murderer would have criminal record. may even spent time in prison. The murderer would target the victim and make the ability to know the victims. The murderer will spend hours, days and maybe weeks. Studying the aspects of each victim. While craving for the womb the murderer desires. As the murderer watches every movement, the victim makes. Study's shown through medical terms. The craving is caused by a cluster of nerve cells lying underneath the cerebral cortex. Releasing dopamine into neuroscientists informing pleasure symptoms like, mouth over watering with saliva, feeling suddenly hungry and having sensational urges. On the other hand. While thinking of the desires. The murderer could feel insomnia causing sleeping pattern to change. Where the murderer is unable to sleep,

Irritability. Where the murderer would be short tempered and break or throw things. A headache from the pressure of thinking and planning. Causing a pressure buildup on the brain and lack of sleep. These are the comment symptoms that the murderer would feel while studying the victim. The murderer will fantasize over the victims. Using a photographic memory. Masturbating while putting the image of the victims eyes. As the victim passes away. Causing a combustion just before ejaculation. Feeling sensational pleasure through the body. This person probably wears a uniform or certain clothing. Appending on which victim. Carring a dark colour bag containing equipment. Needed for completing the job. The murderer would use a form of liquid, as chloroform. Soaked over a rag by knocking the victim unconscious. It does this by given off vapors, that the victim inhales. As the victim breathes in. Through the mouth and nose, causing the victim to panic. feeling stressed and scared. Within less and five minutes the victim will become light headed. Causing a headache and passing out. Moving the victim to a place where the murderer would feel comfortable and pull out the rope from the bag. Tiring up arms and legs of the victim. Stuffing the mouth with a rag. Then tiring another rag around the victims mouth. Playing music, as the murderer uses the blade of the knife to scrape along the edge of the thumb. This probably be the opposite hand. The murderer uses to write with. While watch and waiting till the victim gain's consciousness. Speaking and reassuring the victim before murdering victims".

While sitting listen to the feedback, given by Dr Harpe. Professor Willincole spoke out once Dr Harpe had finished.

"I would like to go and see the crime scene. Where you found the first victim. This will give me a chance to overlook the crime scene. To see if there anything missed. It always best to check the crime scene twice, just in case. I know you had officers go over the area again. But you never know. Dr Harpe will stay and study the letter from the murderer. That might give us some more information on the investigation. So if you ready detective Jones. We'll take a ride down there."

"Yes I ready, will you be ok finding your way back to the investigation room Dr Harpe".

Looking at Dr Harpe as detective Jones spoke. Dr Harpe replied back.

"I should be ok finding my way back to the investigation room. If for any reason I missed a turn or end up in the wrong direction. I should approach someone who works here and ask for their assistant to direct me in the right direction".

Detective Jones pull's up in his car. While the engine was still running. Professor Willincole opens the passenger side door and got in. Clipping the seat belt into place. As they make their way to the crime scene professor Willincole flipped through the pictures of the victim and the area of the crime scene to get a general idea of what the crime scene would look like on the day the victim was discovered. Detective Jones pulled up in the car park at the back of Freeman Street Market. Before entering the crime scene they both popped into the market. Grabbing their take away coffee and sipping the steamy hot coffee with caution to prevent scolding their lips. As they made their way to the crime scene area. Professor Willincole stood looking around the area. Making a mental image in his brain of the night of the murder. Focusing on the mental image. He takes another sip of the coffee and get's detective Jones to follow him. As professor Willincole gives detective Jones his version of the night of the murder.

"I believe the murderer came in a car, with the victim. Who would of been virtually dead or already dead. She would of still been tied up and gagged with plastic covering. To prevent the blood still leaking out. From seeping into the upholstery. The murderer would have parked on the left side of the road opposite the car park. The reason is that, the murderer was not seen on any camera's. The only place where there is a blind spot on the camera's and where the murderer wouldn't been seen by anybody would be the left side of the road. Anywhere else someone would of noticed or the murderer would of been viewed on camera. The murderer would of pulled the victim's body from the boot of the car. Laying it down on the floor.

Unwrapping the plastic cover and dragging the victim off the cover. Folding it up and placing it into the boot of the car. Shutting the boot with one hand. Before dragging the body halfway down the alleyway. The murderer would had to hook both arms. Underneath the victim's armpits. To get the victim to sit upright and moving her leg's so that the victim was balanced. The head of the victim would have tipped to one side. Causing the upper body to slant over. The murderer would have been wearing a plastic cover. To prevent the blood of the victim getting onto the clothes of the murderer. The murderer would of more likely been wearing a hooded jumper to cover the murderer's face just in case. The murderer was seen. The murderer would have left the crime scene and dumped the cover and gloves not far from here. Mmm let's see, that building over there".

Has detective Jones follow's professor Willincole over to the backs of Freeman Street shops. Professor Willincole placed plastic glove onto his hands. Lifted one of the lids of an industrial bin. Using one of his hands, he slowly moved the rubbish. There before their eye's scrunched up in a ball. Where plastic containers containing blood. He placed them into a evidence bag and handed it to detective Jones.

Chapter Eight

PROFILING

The room was filled with people chatting. Slurping drinks as they waited. In the background the clock tick, pinpointing four 'o' clock. As the second hand ticked a few second pass the number twelve. Detective Jones and professor Willincole walked in with a photo of the evidence they had found. While the evidence was being analyzed by the forensic team. Placing it onto the white board. Next to the other evidence. Standing there as he waited for the call. As silence echo through the room. With everyone staring, waiting for detective Jones to speak. Five minutes passed, nothing happened. People sat whispering, wondering why detective Jones had not said anything. As the phone rang just passed, ten pass four. Detective Jones pick up the receiver.

"Hello".

With a man voice coming from the other end of the receiver.

"Can I speak to detective Jones please".

"Speaking".

"Hi detective Jones this is Jeff from the forensic department. We ran some test on the evidence you drop off an hour ago. The plastic scrunch up ball you bag turned out to be a plastic see-through bag. The length of a black bag and two pairs of Vinyl examination gloves. The results show that the blood on the plastic item's are a perfect

80

match to Kayleigh Southan. There was no other evidence inside the gloves of the murderer's DNA. Which means the murderer must of been wearing other gloves. We did analyze under a microscope, marking inside the gloves. Showing that the gloves were some sort of leather. With the see-through bag. There was three holes cut out for the head and arms to go through. It also had a tiny bit of material of blue cotton. That came from a jumper. But no evidence found on DNA. Just a peculiar smell of fragrance".

"Thankyou Jeff".

Placing the receiver back on the phone, looking up at the officers. Before detective Jones started to speak.

"Nice to see everyone turned up on time. That going to save me some paperwork and that one for the record. Don't like to hand out warning. As we are on a very tight schedule. Just a few things to say before I pass you over to professor Wilincole, Dr Harpe and kelly. As you all know tonight a big night. We need to bring down this murderer. Before the murderer strikes. By finding the next victim in question. So far we got a list of single mums with two children, that included Sophie. She doesn't know as it might ruin our chances in catching the murderer. I have detective 'O' Brien and couple of office staking out her address. Just in case, you never know. At this present time Sophia is not home and the officers are still there waiting just in case she come home. Out of the five hundred single mum's. We narrow it down to around fifty single mums living in the Grimsby and Cleethorpes area. Next to a roundabout. The only problem is that we don't have the man power to watch all the fifty single mum's houses. So I am arranging some officers to patrol the areas. Hopefully by doing that we might get luck. By catching the murderer in the act. All fifty woman have been contacted and been told to ring nine, nine, nine. Except a few that didn't answer their phone. That can't be helped and hopefully it not going to be one of them. We have put extra staff on the phone lines, so the lines are free to answer the calls. By linking my mobile with their services. It will automatically send a message straight to my mobile if anything occurs on the case. Which is a good thing as I can send a rapid response. Means we get to the victims house quickly. Cutting out the middle-man, will save time. Next I like to say, the reason for me waiting early. Is the evident me and professor Willincole found. Is a match to the victim blood. The Items we retrieved. Are a see-through plastic bag and a pair of vinyl examination gloves. That was screwed up into a ball and thrown into the industrial waste bins at the back of the Freeman Street shops. The forensic team have examined the items. Which they have found that the murderer was either wearing a jumper or hoodie in the colour of blue and the gloves have inside them. An imprint of some sort leather. So we now know in theory the we looking out for anyone wearing a blue jumper and leather gloves. If you see anyone with that description or acting suspiciously. Stop them in their tracks. Everyone is guilty at this moment in time, till we save that single mum. She is a priority. As I don't want to see the kids lose their mum. I will be sending most of you out on patrol tonight and the one who stay here with be on standby, working the radio's or phones. I now going to pass you over to Professor Willincole and I hope you all brought your little notebooks and you will need to be writing it down. For later reference. Before that take 10 minutes. Get a drink and have a quick smoke. If you smoke. As I need you all alert on this".

After returning from a short break. Professor Willincole stood, leaning onto the desk with his index fingers clenched around the edge of the desk. While speaking to the officers, like he was teaching a class.

"Today I like to discuss profiling. Who can tell me what profiling means. Nobody, ok then Profiling. It reading the sign of the behaviour. That give a logic or summary of the type of person we are looking for. I mean that we base the behaviour. The way the victim was murder and crimes scene. Putting all of the evident together and you will have a realistic idea of the type of person. Who has become a murderer. Another question how many people would a murderer have to murder to become a serial killer. Some people say three, others say five. A serial killer is a person who murders multiple victims with no remorse. That my theory on serial killers. As every serial killer is different with an exception of the ones who copy cat. It goes like this.

We are looking for a person who is in their mid-thirties to early fiftys. This person could be a man or woman who is infertile. They would feel angry, confused and feel different from people around them. The person could have suffered abuse by the mother and for year letting it build up. Till someone or something triggers it and a sudden rush of that hurt and pain hit them like a tonne of bricks. The action of this can affect the motion of the brain. Which bring us to the collusion. The murderer, murderer's women. Taken away the womb of the woman. As a sign of revenge to say if they can't have children, why should the victim. The murderer would be suffering from depression or any kind of mental illness. Making them think if they eat the womb of a young person. It would somehow give them the chance to have children or would be a cure to helping them to be able to have children. Where they become addicted to the tasted. By wanting more, making them kill more frequently. This type of person will not stop till they are caught and feel they are doing justice by making them pay for the suffering they went through. The hair, the murderer sent is a sign of a signature. Like an artist. The murderer feels if they sent the hair it would make them famous by having their nickname plastered all over they newspaper and on the new. Revealing the victim they have murdered, like a piece of art. This is what the murderer would think. While feeling excited like a kid getting a new toy. By using an Indian story is a sign that the murderer is telling you the name that they would like to be called. So asks yourself this question. Why would the murderer give you clues to the next killing? It not that the murderer wants to get caught, it a game. The muderer is playing a game of chess and for every game is one victim. The clue are the moves you would have to think of. To solve the riddle reason I believe the murderer plays the game of chess is that the muderer as given eight clues. Which is what you do in chess. By always thinking eight moves ahead. Another question when someone say two days, no more or no less. You would automactic believe two days fourty eight hours. I spent the last few hours thinking about that. Which bring me to think that the murderer wanted to throw you off the scent. By changing the tactics to the game to make it harder for use to read the murderer's thoughts. This type of person is well educated and more likely would have an intelligent level higher than the average person. The person in mind would be a normal working person someone who would be honest, friendly and trust worthy. They might ever be your friend, family or go to the same church as you. At this time everyone is a likely subject, you, me and everyone one you know. That makes this person very dangers, not just women. I believe if a man intervene. The murderer will attack. So don't think the murderer will come easily. As the murderer will take as many of you. As the murderer can. We need to take the murderer down quickly and by not end the life of the murderer. Just disable one of the murderer's limbs will be enough to slow them down and stop them in their tracks.

As professor Willincole finished off, what he was saying. Dr Harpe jumped straight in. Placing the letter onto the projector. So the letter projected onto the white screen that Dr Harpe setup before the profiling began.

"I just like everyone to take a look at the screen. Where I projected the letter. As you can see how the murderer curves. Script font certain letters, a, c, d, f, g, i, j, k, n, q, r, s, t and y. Also all letters are upper cut. Meaning capital lettering. Last of all, if you look closely in between the lines. You can notices, smudged along the letter is ink. This implies, the murderer is lefthanded. In medical terms a person who is left-handed will find it hard to use certain equipment. Example scissor, peelers and writing. Why did I say writing. The reason is left handed people write against the letters and this causes the letters to smudged. Getting into the letter and the meaning of the way the murderer implies their self. Notices how the murderer know detective Jones first name. By calling him detective Jones and changing it. Two things, first thing. Dimension, the murderer want full control. By telling detective Jones that they want, will and are. Example hostage situation. By not putting hostages into danger you will be obeying the terrorist rules. This is what we have here, even know detective Jones is not a hostage. The murderer is still taking control. Second thing, the murderer would have knew detective Jones as a friend, sale person or a professional health care. Other would be stalking, going through the bin and investigating background on detective Jones. The murderer is calling is work, artwork and changes his mind quite a lot. Making the murderer very undetectable. Not knowing what way the murderer will decided. The murderer stood around watching the crime scene. Which would have been from a distance. By given the full view of the crime scene. Making sure the murderer was able to view detective Jones every move. As the murderer mentioned every little detail detective Jones did at the crime scene. The murderer believes that it was one of their best art pieces. They had every done. By calling it the most beautiful work. Shows that the murderer has no remorse or feelings over the victim. This can mean a number of things, hate, no relation, mental illness or look alike. In most cases it turns out to be psychological changed within the behaviour. causing the person to trigger and start murdering victim. This maybe caused by something happening in their childhood. Which is then repeats itself in adulthood. Example as a child the person could have got psychological abuse. Which doesn't affected the behaviour. But then would have a simular affected that would trigger the behaviour. Changing the way the person would act. That affects behavioral neuroscience. changing the brain patten of thinking. As you can see that the murderer would listen to music. It knows that music helps you to relax, think and concentrate. By given you more focus. The murderer also shows anger as the victim's screams. Making it hard to hear the music. Causing the murderer to stuff a cloth into the victim's mouth. To fade out the sound of screaming. This means the murderer would had gone through the experience. Where the parents would have shouted at each other a lot. So as a child, the murderer would have hidden and turned up t.v. or stereo to block out the sound of the parents. By grabbing hold of the hair tight. Rocking back and forward. In a sitting position, with legs crunch up to the chest. Shout out over and over again please stop. While tightly closing eyelids together. Notice here how the murderer gets a thill better than sex. As the murderer looks into the victim's eyes. Medical term is that at this point the chemical within the brain combust, exploding cause every nerve in the body to have a sensational feeling. Example like when you fall in love, as you make first eye contact. Given you butterfly in the stomach. You can see here the murderer try's to make a joke out of the hair. Then reveals that it's for us to know every victim murder by the murderer. This is know as the signature. As every murderer will have a different way of murdering their victims and leaving a signature to say that they murdered this victim. The murderer then goes on to give us clues and writes it in a riddle. I have highlighted every clue in the letter. Given use eight clues. One of them clues does interest me. That the murderer takes an organ and fry it for their lunch. As we know the organ that was missing from the victim was the womb. In some cases there is always a reason for this. I believe that the mother would have left the murderer at a very young age. Making the murderer as a kid to rebel against the situation. Then over time a build up of hate, anger and depression. I believe that the partner would of broken up with the murderer. Maybe even taken away the children. This could of been the trigger. causing the murderer to start murdering the victims. By taking away the womb from the woman. Would be to pervent the woman from having children. The murderer would believe the woman to be a resemblance to their mother. Feeling resembles against their mother and withdrawing the womb by preventing birth from carring on. By accidentally eating the womb. Gives the person a taseted for it. Taking the hair of would stop the spirit going into heaven. This takes me to the end of the letter where the murderer makes sure. They are called the scalp slayer. In theory the indian story was about an indian belief. When a warrior kills another warrior. They would slice the hair from the top of the head. know as the scalp of the head. To prevent the spirit being pulled into heaven. Going by the letter I believe the muderer was not well educated and may be behind on subjects. Over time the murderer would of taught their self and gained more knowledge after leave school".

After Dr harpe had finished. Detective Jones gave the comand for the psychic to do her reading on the murderer.

"Hi everyone, the thieves I getting from the case. Is that dark spirit around this person. It not a good spirit nooo. Evil, very evil spirit. This person has been through a lot of pain and heartache over many years. Making them suffer and feel hatriage against the female sex. But there also a feeling of Love and hate between someone. This person not a woman, it seems to be a man that is causing the love and hate within this dark spirit. I feel that the person in question, believe's that by taking away the womb will replenish the sins and take away evil. By cooking and eating the womb. Serving it with veg and gravy. Liking the taste. Something about this person. They feel sorry for the victims. Maybe abit of guilt has they comforted the victims. I see a room with two long drak brown settlies. Which is very over crowded with junk. This room is kept pretty clean and tidy. Even know there not much space to move around. Something going to happen, something bad. I feel it in my bones and that shriver down the back of my spine. Yes this is the place where the victim dies. Oooh the pain, THE PAIN, THE PAIN. I feel the blade, slicing through my belly and the pain is unbearable. Why why meee!, I feel a tugging, pulling and my inside stretching. I just can't see the person's face, it all a blurr. There is something I focusing on an object, a clock. It wooden with flowers carved into the clock. That has a wooden doors where the robin pops out of every hour after a number of bells to the time on the clock. Attached to a thin metal arm, make a sound of the robin. I see the time eight twenty-five. Yes the big hand is on the five and the small hand is just passed the eight. I have nothing else, I need to sit I feel weak".

As one of the officers places a chair behind the psychic she flops down resting and feel tired from the ordeal. Detective Jones finished the profileing meeting.

"I just Like to say thank you for that and Just over their by the refreshment table their a list of duties with everyone's name of which duties you all been allocated for tonight. Please check them before leaving thank you that all for now."

Chapter Nine

TIME UP

As the night creeps in, a calm wind blow and sound of cars driving by. While a middle age woman sits holding a mug with her both hand. Sipping her hot drink as the steam from her drink suppresses her skin. A person sits in a dark vehicle from the otherside of the road. Starring at the window from the otherside of the road. That had curtain shut. Making the light shine from the sides of the window. Tapping the index fingers on the steering wheel, with both hands. Before deciding to pull the door handle and exit out of the vehicle. Inserting the key into the keyhole of the trunk. Pulling out a tool box containing different departments. Shutting the trunk has they walk towards the house. Standing there for a split second. Just before pushing the doorbell with their index finger closest to their thump. She sits forward puzzled. Thinking who would be coming around at this time. Placing the mug down onto the coffee table. Using both arms to push herself up and walk to the door.

The woman had mousse curly blond hair that came down past her shoulders. Put into a bobble style. She had blue eyes, with long eyelashes that were hardly noticeable. High cheek bones and chin that had been broken perversely. Causing the chin to stick in and making the top of her mouth to stick out with her top teeth showing. Her skin was pale white and she never used makeup. Wearing red pyjamas with pattens all over them and a white furry dressing gown. With the belt of the dressing gown tied into a bow. She had thick furry colourful socks and white slippers. Just around her neck an neckless containing an gold heart. That open up showing small pictures of her children.

As the person stood waiting for the door to open they pull out a small brown bottle from the pocket. Using the constants they slipped the liquid form onto a rag that was wrapped around the brown bottle and placing the bottle back into the pocket, they pulled it from. Holding the rag tight in the palm of their hand. Then placing the hand into the pocket by making sure the woman wouldn't notice. As the clicking sounds came from the other side of the door. The woman unbolts the locks and turns the door handle. Pulling the door open. She peeked her head around the edge of the door with the chain still attached. Eyeballing the person up and down. She notices a person stood wear a dark grey jumpsuit holding the toolbox in their right hand with the left hand hidden in the jumpsuit pocket. Before she spoke out.

"Can I help you".

"Sorry to bother you madame. I just need to check your phone line. I from British Telecom and someone just smashed the telephone box. So I need to check if your phone is back online. Before I confirm the job complete".

"Just wait there I go and check it".

She shut the door and walk over to the telephone. Picking it up and listen for a tone on the phone. Nothing, dead as a whistle. Placing the phone back she opens the door. Taking the chain off.

"No it not, there no tone. It completely dead".

"That ok madame, not a problem. All I need to do is use my little computer device and I should have your phone line back on. I only need to check your phone box connector. Where your phone is plugged in. Which will take me no longer than ten minutes".

"Well it is a bit late. But I do need the phone on just in case someone needs to get in touch. Are you sure it just take ten minutes".

"Yes".

As she stood Sucking on her top lip. Given that thinking look on her face. For a while before given an answer.

"Ok, if it only going to be ten minutes. It is better that you get it done now. Instead of me having to wait for you to come back".

As the person walk into the house standing and watching the woman close the front door. Putting the chain back on. Letting the woman walk in front as she showed the person the way. Pulling out their left hand from the pocket. The person unravels the rag. While walking behind. Wrapping their arm around the woman. Placing the rag over the woman mouth and nostrils. She put a fright up, struggling to break free. As she begins to feel light headed. While her fights to break free weakens. She blacks out. The person carefully places the woman onto the floor. Before grabbing her under the shoulders. Dragging the woman body into the front room. Then going back into the hallway to grab the toolbox. They had carefully place down without making a sound. Before grabbing the woman with their arm. Opening a few departments on the toolbox. Pulling out a folded plastic sheet, two ropes, some more rags, pair of leather gloves, disposable apron and large gloves. Last of all two knives, one sheathed and the other a surgery knife. Placing all the items onto the brown carpet. While laying out the plastic sheet. The person put on their apron, leather gloves and large gloves over the top. Rolling the woman body onto the sheet. Tiring the arms and legs with the ropes. Using one rag crunch up into a ball and stuffing it into the mouth of the woman. Tiring the other rag that was placed around the mouth at the back of the head. The person then life the woman. Placing the head against the dark brown three seater settee. So the woman was slumped up slightly where she was laying with her head upright. The person stands up and creeps upstairs. Using the same rag they used on the woman and some more of the liquid from the brown bottle. Going into the kids rooms and place the rag over their mouths and nosrals, one at a time. While the children slepted. Inhaled the fumes. Falling into a deep sleep. Making them unable to hear or responded to any sound coming from downstairs. As the person enter back into the front room. They walk over to the stereo picking up the cd. That were stacked on each other. Flicking thought them till the right one came along. Answering to what the person throught of each cd. While throwing the unwanted cd over their right shoulder. Causing the cases to break in half and the cd to roll around, before coming to a halt.

"Crap, crap, seriously, bad taste, oh my fucking god. Please don't tell me you have no taste in music, wait. Interesting I do like this one. Let see is this the type of music to fit my work of art?. Yep it will do, can't be asked going through any more".

Placing the cd into the stereo. Pressing play and then turning the volume down by not causing a disturbance. Just enough so that it would cut out the sound of screaming. While the person fulfilled their art piece when they slice the flesh with the sharp knife. Sitting on the dark brown chair opposite the woman. Waiting for her to come around. With their legs crossed, holding the surgery knife they pick up. Scrapping the sharp end of the knife across the right hand thumb. Putting no pressure on the knife. So it wouldn't draw blood. Just sending the thump reddish. From the sharpness of the blade. As she opens her eyes. Everything was blurred at first. With her head thumping and filling very confused. Not knowing where, who or what time or day it was. This went on for about half an hour. Before she released what was going on. While laid, feeling scared and shivering. Even though the room temperature was very warm. The shock of what was happening around her. She layed there with fear for her kids. Has she didn't care for herself. Trying to say "please don't". With tears rolling down both sides of her face. That came out muffled. With no word understood or heard. Watching the woman. The person saw the tears run down the side of her face. They know it was time, as they stood up and walked over to the woman. Kneeling down and before removing the rags from the mouth of the women. The person speaks calmly. As they look into the woman eyes.

"Scream and I will cut your tounge out. shh don't cry I promise no harm will come to your children. You have my word".

"Please, please don't. Why are you doing this. Let me go and I won't tell a soul I promise. I too young to die. My children need me. I'm all they have in life, they need me".

As she lay trembling with her heart racing. She could feel every beat. Knowing that she will never see her children grow and never be there for their birthdays, Christmas, marriage and her grand children that they have in the future. The bigger worry she had was. Would this person keep to their promise or is that a lie to make her think the children will be fine. Maybe the person was saying this just to keep her calm and when they had finished, her children would be next. Placing the index finger closest to the thumb on the left-hand onto her lips and put right-hand index finger onto their lips. To say stop talking. So that the person could have their say before they continued.

"Shh, just listen that all you have to do. It not you, it just I need what you contain inside. Everything will be ok. I ensure you that the pain will only last a little time. You will die, it up to you to make this easy or hard. Even way I will get what I have come for. Then you be able to rest in peace. One thing I must tell you is that you will not go to heaven, no. As I believe, you are a sinner. You have had both children without getting married. This means I will have to remove the hair from the head to prevent you from being pulled into heaven. You will pay for your sins, believe me. Yes, all you woman are the same. First with eve, then with the very person I cherish and loved. Yes, I talking about my dear own mother. Who I could never forgive. I won't go on about her. Then their you. I know I said it was nothing to do with you. that I meant. Like I say I don't know you from Adam. but I have studied you and learnt about your dirty little sin. So like I say it not you. It the sins you carry within you and for this you have to pay the price. Let me tell you a little story. Before nite, nite ha ha ha!. Two days ago I gave the police plenty of time to track you down. What do they do. I tell you nothing. The bloody pigs just sat there. Scratching the top of their heads trying to work out the clues to the letter I sent them. It was easy, even a five year old would of work it out. These so call protectors of the community. Would have the clues smack them in the face and properly still wouldn't have worked the answer out. It so simply, think like chess. I gave them eight clues. So it looks like I won this one. The so call police, what a wasted of space. line the fucks up and shoot the lot of them. Ha ha ha!, that would make my day. Just think about it, give me the giggles. Anyway you know what. They spend hundreds, maybe thousand of taxpayers money. Putting a five to ten-minute broadcast on tv, for what. Someone to come forward. Wait maybe me, not!. To top it off the stupid wankers. You don't mind me using few word do you?. Just nod your head for yes or no. great I please you don't mind. Right the stupid wankers sit outside a single mum. That work and date the detective who is in charge of this case. Thinking I am stupid enought to go there. In their dreams. No not my type. She hasn't got that sweet tasting meat that I hunger for. Yes I eat human wombs, only from the sweet smell I get. You got that sweet smell that makes my mouth water. She had the dead smell on her. That puts me off. Think about it, that woman works with dead people. Even know she showers every day, the smell lingers. I tell you what it smells like, rotten meat. Just thinking about it make me feel sick. Now you understand why I have to keep you alive. Two reasons, first reason. The meat tastes even more sweeter and the second reason. The smell when a person body shuts down give off a sweet buttery smell. That only last a little time. Which is enought time to take the hair off and dump the body before that dead smell comes. I must say you have beautiful curly hair, that I love. Something the police don't know is that I keep a peace of the hair that I take off and placed it into my book. That has a picture of you. Yes, I did take pictures of you and your children. While I sat in my car watching you do your day to day activities. You must know what I do with the rest of the hair, cause you do. They boardcasted it nationwide on t.v. For their own enjoyment. I will give them credit for one clue. They got the name I wanted right. I am the one the only. Living scalp slayer and I will live up to my name. Ho yes, I will. So every person out there will honor and repact me. As I will walk the hall of fame. Well is that the time, we best get started. Like I say we don't want to be late for the ball, do we now. Don't cry, it all be over soon".

Her eyes widen. While her whole body shakes with fear as the person open her dressing gown. Lifting the pyjamas top above her belly button. Pulling down the bottom, just enough so her private part where still covered with the pubic hair just showing. The person grabs the surgery knife and pierced the skin open from the right side of the stomach. Across to the left. Just below the belly button. Causing the intestines to spill out. She screamed as the blade ran through the flesh. From the pain that sent her whole body into shock causing the body to stiffen. With her eyes filling up with tears. That ran down her face that much the side of her hair became wet. Feeling tired and dehydrated, with the surroundings from her eye sight slowly getting darker. As she passes out from the pain and loss of blood. Which surrounded her in a form of a puddle. With parts bright red and other parts thick dark red. almost the colour of black. The person then cut. Using the belly button as a guideline. Downwards, millimeters from the top of the private part and upwards. Stopping just below the belly button. Pushing their hand into the open area. Stretching the sides. Till the organs appear. Using the surgery knife. The person cut's just above the Virginia and cuts away each fallopian tube. Before removing womb and placing it into a container. Putting into the top department of the toolbox. They then carefully push the intestines back into the open area. pulling the top down and the bottoms up. Closing the dressing grow. Tiring the belt into a knot. Picking up the scraped knife. Holding the hair up has they saw into the flesh of the scalp and guild the knife around the bone. Till the skin separates. Leaving the skull appearing. Without taking care when removing the hair and skin. Sealing it into a large freezer bag and resting it on the container holding the womb. By this time the woman body had shut down. with her finger tip and feet turning colour. Has the person packs the items used into the toolbox. While moving the plastic sheet from underneath the woman. Her head tiles to the right. Causing the brain fluid that was building up inside the ear to Drains out. Picking up the toolbox the person exit the building.

Placing the toolbox back in the trunk of the car. Sitting in the car they pull out a mobile phone from the glove department. Knowing it might be a long time before the children awake. so they decided to make the call. While still wearing the leather glove dialing nine, nine, nine.

"Hello operator. Which service you require".

"Police please".

"Putting you through".

"Police service".

"You have to come. I hear screaming coming from the house on the corner of Devon-port drive it by roundabout. Please hurry I think someone murdering her".

As they drive off, throwing the mobile phone into someone front yard. Further down the road.

Chapter Ten

VICTIM TWO

Detective Jones sat in his offices going through the evident to see if he had missed something. Sat on the other side of the desk was professor Willincole and Dr Harpe. Waiting to hear back from the officers that were out looking for the murderer. Sergeant cook walks down the corridor. Stopping outside detective Jones office. He knocks on the door waiting for an answer from the other side.

Sergeant cook was a young officer. With short dark black hair. He had blue eyes, button nose and a dimple in the middle of his chin. The face was long with stubble and the left ear had a gold stud in. He was tall and skinny, with a limp when he walked. Wearing neatly pressed white shirt, with two black bages that contain golden bags. The golden badges were three numbers and two stripes. His black trousers had a black belt that was hidden by the shirt being tucked in and pulled out slightly so it hangs over. Just on his right side. Hooked on to the trousers was a walkies talky. That had a receiver connected to a black curly wire. Which hooked onto the right shirt pocket. The shoe were black steel toe caps. That shined and reflected the light of them.

"Come in".

Detective Jones shout out. As the door open halfway. Sergen cook still holding the handle with one hand and the other against the door frame, has he spoke.

"Sir, there's been another murder. We had a nine, nine, nine call and when the officers went to investigate. They found a body of a middle age woman. Try contacting you by your mobile but you weren't answering. So they asked to try your office to see if you were in".

"Where about".

"Devon-port Drive, sir. The house was also next to the roundabout and two kids were found unconscious in their bedrooms".

Ok, let the officers on scene know. Not to touch anything and I am on my way. Sophia, is she....?".

Ok, sir I will do. She fine sir, managed to get hold of her, not long ago. Apparently she was out at her girlfriends house and quite shock to see the officers parked outside her house".

Detective Jones let a big relieve off, knowing Sophia was safe from any harm.

"Thankyou sergeant Cooks".

Detective Jones vehicle pulls up outside the victims house. With half of the street lit up by flashing blue lights. Stepping out of the vehicle with him was professor Willincole and Dr Harpe. While detective 'O' Brien appears from nowhere to give him the update of the murder victim.

"Sir, I arrived about twenty minutes ago. Spoke to the two offices, Rose and Detroit. They found a middle age woman in the front room. Murdered and the two children both girls not responding to anything we tryed. They both were in their bedrooms. The oldies in the middle bedroom and young's in the back bedroom unconscious. one eleven and other two. The crime scene officer she is already here. Followed me when I got the call on the car radio. She taking photos at the moment".

As the detective Jones speaks out".

"Is it the same as the last one."

Detective 'O' Brien reply's back. With both detective talking while the other two listen to what was being said.

"Yes, Hair removed from top of head and blood seeping though the dressing gown. Around the stomach area".

"And the children".

"Ambulance pick them up, ten minutes ago. They have been taken to Grimsby hospital. Officer Wilson and officer Vincent are waiting there. For feedback from the hospital and social services has been informed. They sending a social care officer to the hospital to speak to the older girl, when she awakens".

"Ok thanks, I need you to go to the hospital as you will need to speak to the social service officer". As I don't want them to talk to the girl. It will be better coming from you. We need to see if the girl remembers anything that could help with the case".

"Yes sir".

At that point detective 'O' Brien made her way to the hospital. While Professor Willincole and Dr Harpe went around looking at the crime scene. Trying to image murder scene in their heads. Detective Jones went to see the crime scene officer. As Sophia stood pushing the button on the camera, the flash lit the room and blinded you for a split second. A tap on her right shoulder made her jump. Turning around with her palm against her chest as she notices detective Jones standing before her.

"Detective Jones!, you gave me a heart attack. Creeping up on me like that".

Given her the puppy look.

"Sorry my love, needed to get your attention. How are you and the kids doing".

"We ok, how you doing".

"Fine and that question you ask me".

"Yes go on".

With a puzzled look on Sophia face. As she was not expecting detective Jones to be answering the question at this point of time.

"It was to do with the situation that happens earlier. That got me thinking about the question".

Standing there feeling very blushed and hot in the face as detective Jones spoke. While Sophia butted in on a couple detective Jones words.

"What situation".

"It hard to say, at this point in time".

"Right, would it be to do with the time you had that letter".

"Yes, that it. well here it go's. I have been thinking about the question and let not be boyfriend and girlfriend or have an engagement. Why don't we just get married. After this case, when we get more time for each other".

With tears streaming down Sophia face. Holding her right hand over face as she covers her mouth and nose. Then suddenly throwing herself at detective Jones. Wrapping her arms around him. Then whispering into the left ear, of detective Jones. While the tears dampen the collier of his shirt.

"Yes, Yes!. I will marry you, your my world".

While everyone stood around ear-wigging on what detective Jones was saying. Totally surprised in what detective Jones came out with. As they knew him as a person. Who would never do something like this. Thinking to themselves, "Is he feeling ok". While being happy for him. But more happier for Sophia for getting what she wanted from detective Jones. They all know about them two and Sophia had talked to the odd one within the police forces. Which went around the whole police station without getting back to detective Jones. At the same time detective Jones was thinking in his head. As he done the right thing. Especially standing in some dead woman house. While on a case, stood over the victims body. Sophia unwrapped her arm and wiped away the tears from her cheeks with the arm of the protected white hooded jumpsuit.

"I bested get on, I call you over when I ready to give you report".

"Yep, I think I need a smoke. Get one of the officers to grab me. I'll be sitting in my car waiting".

"Ok, Could you just wait there for a minute, I just got to get something from the van and I don't want your officer accidently stepping on the crime scene that might damage any evidence".

"Ok".

Sophia, disappeared for a couple of minutes, before coming back holding some more evidence bags in her hand.

The room was narrow and long, with cream walls. Textured style ceiling and a light that hung on a wire. With a beige lamp shade. The two doors on the left side of the room. That where a metre apart from each other. The one at the back left corner of the room was connected to the kitchen and the other one in centre left of the room was connected to the hallway. It was very cluttered with toys. That where packed away tidily. With a two piece suite. A three seater and a chair. Between the settee and the chair, was a wooden coffee table. That had glass in the centre. Just to the left was an old coal fire. With a copper bucket that contained coal. A poker stick and shovel, that was also copper. The flat screen telly sat underneath the window. Containing brown curtains. Which went behind the telly, resting onto the floor. At the back of the room. Opposite the kitchen door. Was a couple of shelves. That had a stereo and music disks on. With the speakers hanging on the wall just above. Some of the compact disks were laying on the floor. Beside there broken cases.

Detective Jones walks to the car and sits in the drive's seat. Door slightly open, Sparking up the fag from the glove department that detective Jones pulled out of the open pack. That he left in there a few day ago. With every drag he takes from the cigarette. Trying to blow smoke rings and failing most of the time. With only the odd one. Not even noticing on the back seat of his car a shoe box contain a red ribbon tied neatly around the shoe box. Into a bow at the top of the box. The door open, with one of the twin police officer stick his head in.

"Sir, your lady of the night is ready for you. May I say you hit a winner there, sir".

"Less of your cheek and tell her I'm on my way".

While he takes the last few drags from the cigarette. As it slightly burns the butt by burning the sides of detective Jones index fingers. Detective Jones stubs the fag out, into the full ashtray in the car. That was spilling ash from other cigarettes. That was overflowing the sides of the ashtray. Closing the car door, not even locking it. He walks back into the house. Pulling out the little black notebook and opening it to a clean page, before speaking to Sophia.

"What do we have then".

Looking at Sophia as she begin's to speak.

"We have a woman who been killed the same way as the first victim. She has been dead for a couple of hours. With the hair removed from the top of the head. causing the brain fluid to seep out of one of the ears. Also the stomach has been punctured and the same knives have been used. A shattered used on the head and the sharp pointed knife used on the stomach".

While Sophia pointed them out. Detective Jones clicked his pen and jotted it down.

"Do we have a name for the victim".

"I believe so, I took the name from one of the letters that was laying about. Her name is Miss Donna Mroczkowska. Don't worry it was from an open gas bill. That was sent this month. As I do know over previous occupants sometimes have mail sent".

"What about the age of the victim".

"Yes, I have that. I open the purse of her. To check for other detail on the victim. Found a birth certificate. Which it quite strange for a person to keep something that important in her purse. Maybe she been out or needed it for identification. It states she is forty-one year old".

"So she polish".

"No, she was born in Grimsby. Maybe one of her parents is polish or both".

"Right, ok then".

As detective Jones closes his small black notebook. Placing it into his pocket of his coat. Professor Willincole and Dr Harpe came over to discuss the theory on the crime scene. While professor Willincole started, Dr Harpe views the victim. That had been moved. So the victim was laid with her head rested on the carpet floor.

"Hi, you must be Sophia. Detective Jones has told me so much about you. I am Professor Willincole. Which you be seeing alot of on this case. Well detective Jones, I had a look around and this is what I come up with on the crime scene. The person would have turned up in a uniform, gas and eletric person, meter reader, sale person or telecom person. I going to say it would of been telecom. The reason for this is the woman telephone line is dead. So I took a look through the bills. Came across a bank statement and notice the woman paid her bills by direct debits. Which clearly shows the phone bills been pay for this month. They would have gained the trust of the woman. By letting them in. The person would have waited for the right time. Before knocking the victim out with the liquid fumes. They would have dragged the women body over to the sofa. Putting her in a sitting position. Tying her up, then would have gone to the children rooms and used the liquid fumes so that they would not wake up during the murder. I believe that the person went over to the woman music disks. Throwing the album that they didn't like onto the floor and playing the one that they wanted to listen to while murdering the woman. So I open the compact disk draw on the stero system. Which had trances music disk in it. The person wouldn't of play it very loud, no. The person would of play it just enough to dime out the sound of the victim screaming. While opening the stomach. They would have sat in the other chair. Opposite the victim. Waiting for them to awake. So the person would then speak before carrying on with the murder".

Dr harpe stood up. Turned around facing the three of them to begin his say his theory on the murder. While the three of them turn there focus onto Dr Harpe. Still with difficulty taking every word in.

"Good evening madam. It so nice to finally meet you. Sophia isn't it, yes. I'm Dr Harpe and my role is a graphologist. I believe that the victim been dead for just over couple hours now. In medical terms, a person's body will shut down and hearing is the last thing to go. In some cases the victim could still be hearing everything going on around them. It takes up to approximately twenty-four hours for rigor mortis to completely set in. During this time the body will drop in temperature. Starting from fingertips and toes. Gradually working it way through the body. As every hour passes. Another part of the body will go cold and stiffen. As you can see hear the woman. Know as the victim. Has started to stiff in certain parts, hands, arms, feet and legs. Taken all this into a count. Using a mathematics terms. In the first hour the fingertips and toes, turns a blueish purple colour and coldness set in. From there it slowly creeps up the legs and down the arms. Causing the arms and legs to stiffen. Which means that rigor mortis would have set into the arms and legs by two hours. I also notice's the forehead has started dropping in temperature. Which brings me to the conclusion that the victim as been dead for two hours twelve minutes precisely. Due to the cells of the brain electricity breaking down completely. Making the head part drop in temperature, rigor mortis then set in making the joints to lock in the position. This bring's me to thinking. If the victims dies just over two hours. A call was made to nine, nine, nine. That would of took about fifteen minutes for the police officers to radio throught and the information to be passed onto you. Around ten minutes to get ready to leave the police station. Twenty minutes to arrive on scene. Forty-five minutes from there. If my calculation is right that's only hour and a half. Which means the call had been made forty-five minutes after the victim died. According to the officer at the desk as we left. He said that on the phone call the woman was screaming and the person who call also said they think someone murdering her. By summon this up. I believe the call was made from the murderer. The only problem is the voice was computerised. Making it harder to pin down the voice of the murderer. I believe it can be done through analyzing. But this will take weeks or maybe months. Which we don't have time. Before the murderer strikes again. Something else came into mind. The murderer is very neat and tidy. According to scientifically we might be looking for a woman murderer. As it very rare for a man to clean up after them self. I could be wrong. But I certain we are looking for a woman murderer".

At this point detective Jones said his last peace before he was ready to leave with the two agents from the M.I.5.

"Well someone been doing their homework. You lots of officers, except Sophia and professor Willincole. Should take a leaf out of Dr Harpe book. I see you later Sophia and wait for the evidence. As I have an appointment with my computer to type the report up".

While getting into detective's Jones vehicle. Dr harpe passed the shoe box over to detective Jones.

"Detective Jones you have a parcel on your back seat. It looks like the same one from the murderer".

With the blood draining from his face. As detective Jones takes the shoe box of Dr Harpe. Looking around with a vacant look on his face.

"The murderer been heard. this is what I received after the first murdered victim. Officers search the area. The murderer been back and left another shoe box".

Shouting out that loud half the street could hear detective Jones. With his heart racing and his palms sweating. Detective Jones slowly open the box. That was now resting on the bonnet of the vehicle. While removing the letter. Leaving the rest of the contents of the shoe box and passing the box to an officer. To give to Sophia. Detective Jones and the two agents stood there reading the letter.

> "Hello Chris,
>
> I do miss these little moments. Me writing love letters to you and you reading them. Anyway got you a present. Another wig for your bald head. Opp's done it again. I must stop taken the piss out of you. As I stand watching you clean my art away. I think about the woman. Ho god do I think about it. With my whole body tingling with excitement. It the eyes, you just got to look into them. I let you into a secret of mind. It started as a child. Yes life been hard growing up. Still until this day the memory's still haunt me. That all I will tell you today. Maybe next time I give you a little more. Getting back to, you know what I going to say. Yes, the clue's and hear it go's.
>
> As I drive to my house, where my husband and two children live. Somewhere in Grimsby. Not that far from the hospital. It begins to get dark. As night pulls in. Sitting there in my car. I turn the key in the ignition. An arm wraps around me. Covering my face with a rag. While filling light headed. My eye shut upon me.

Wakening in a car park with my hands and legs tightened. While listen to the person. Here it comes pain, tears and then it time to leave without saying goodbye. To my family or my friends.

There you go you now have you next set of clues, to work on. Maybe this time you will be on time. I give you two days, no more, no less. The clock as started ticking. Will you save her or will you not.

Your Sincerely
The Scalp Slayer

Chapter Eleven

THE CHILDREN

Detective 'O' Brien sit waiting in the waiting room of the hospital. With her right leg cross over the left leg. Resting a magazine on top. While holding the edges of the pages with both hands. reading stories, waiting to interview the older child. As the handle of the door turned. An oldish woman enters and sits down opposite. While detective 'O' Brien lift's her head watching as the lady sits down. Placing her leather attache case onto the floor by her legs. Before she introduced herself.

The lady had light grey short hair with purple highlights. Which was tightly permed. Her eyes were blue. Wearing glasses that had half shape lens. That rested on the tip of her nose. With a mole just on the left side of her nose. The lady face was chubby and whiteish from the foundation. With roses red lips stick on her lips. She spoke very posh in a hushed way. With her nostils flaring as the lady moved her lips. Just below her chin. Another mole with little bits of hair sticking out of the top of the mole. She had gold earrings in both ears and a peal neckless, contain fake peals. The lady had a flowery blouse. Contain the colours of gold and brown. Wearing a grey checked suit jacket and skirt. That had light brown lines within the suit. Clipped to the jacket of the suit, onto the pocket was an identification badge. The lady was only five foot tall and chubby. With oversize breasts causing the white bra to appear through the gap of the blouse and the button just about holding the blouse together. From the tightness as the blouse fitted around. She had black high heel shoes. Which made her wobble slightly as she walked and white tights, pulled above her hips.

"Hello, I'm Mrs Thelma bagshaw. I am assuming you are detective 'O' Brien?. Who I was informed of meeting you here by my mobile phone a few minutes ago. They said that I am just to take notes as you be conducting the interview with the older child. I from Child Social Care. Department of Social Services and will be in charge of the children's welfare. When they leave the hospital. As their social worker".

Shutting the magazine detective 'O' Brien placed both hands on top of the magazine. interlocking her index fingers as she replied.

"Yes, I am detective 'O' Brien. I was also informed I would be meeting someone from Social Services. As I am the one interview the oldish girl. You be representing her. Has the father whereabouts is unknown and the girl will need an adult present, during the interview".

"Yes, I understand that and the department are looking into that. To try and relocate the father or any relative the children are able to stay with. Otherwise the children will have to be placed in care. Which we don't want to do. As it better for the children to be with people they know. Than being placed in care with total strangers, disrupt the schooling".

"Yes, I agree. So if any information on the children relative or father comes up. I be please to inform you and fax you the information over".

"That be wonderful. Well just dial the Social Service department and the extension number which is four, four, one, two on the fax. This will come straight through to the office. As the building is also part of the council offices. Do you have a fax number incase we come across information the police may require".

"Yes, dial the Grimsby police station. Extension number one, nine, two. That will come directly to my office department. The same number and tell the operator extension number one, nine, eight will put you through to me or if I am out the operator will take a message and I will get back to you".

A young age woman opens the door holding a clipboard and a stethoscope around her neck. Short and medium weight. Her black hair was tucked into a green hairnet. overlapping the woman ears. she had dark brown eyes, tanned skin and chubby cheeks. Wearing a green surgery top, hat and trousers. White coat with pens sticking out of the top pocket of the white coat. Clip to the white coat was a name badge on one side and on the other side was a silver fob watch. That was cover by the clipboard. As she rests it against her chest. With the paperwork clipped between the coat and the clipboard. Shaken the Social workers hand and then the detective 'O' Brien hand. While she was talking.

"I am Dr Soloman. I see you both have got to know each other. Well that saved me a job. I don't have to introduce you to each other. Both girls are stable and awake. Recovered very well. I just like to keep them here for one night to observe. Before I discharge them over to you Mrs bagshaw and detective 'O' Brien, I have a report written up the time you finished interviewing the child. I will say this if it gets too much for the girl. I while personally stop you interviewing and I will cut the interview short. As the children health is my up most importance while under my care. does anyone have a problem with that?."

both of them said "No" and Dr soloman then carried on speaking.

"I been running tests on the children. There no trace of the chemical left in their system. The children have been clear for about an hours. They still fill nauseous and the two year old as been sick couple of times. I gave them both pain relief for their headaches. Also to make the children comfortable. They have been moved out of trauma toward B. Place into a room together and are just having something to eat and drink. So if you ready, I take you both to see them. I'll be keeping a close watch while the interview is being taken. One more thing, forty-five minutes ago two officers arrived. Which are sat just outside the door of the children room. As I spoken to detective Jones on the phone earlier. Requesting he would like officers there on guard for the children safety. Which got me, they were already here before detective Jones rang. He said he knows you are dealing with this part of the investigation and don't feel like the children are in any danger. It just a precaution and he waiting to hear the results back from you detective 'O' Brien. If you follow me I take you down to the B ward where the children are".

As both women follow the doctor down the corridors into the lift. Getting off on the second floor. Till they came to a double door with a pin code with a wash basin at the side. White bin containing a yellow bag next to the wash basin. Just above was a soap dispenser, paper towels and a bottle of anti-bacteria gel that rested on the wash basin just between the taps. Washing their hands, then squirting the bacteria gel onto their hands by rubbing them together before the doctor punch the code. Into the pin code as they entered the B ward where the girls were. While walking on passing a number of doors. They came to a corridor that ran across. On the left was a reception area and just to the right on the same side was two officers standing either side of a door that had a window with blinds still drawn. The officers on the right side of the door. Opened the door, greeting detective 'O'Brien as the three of them entered.

The Room was average size. White with two hospital bed that had cot side. A television between both beds and lamps just above both beds attached to arms. That came from a white electric board which ran across the wall just above the beds containing sockets and hospital equipment. On each side of the beds was an electrocardiogram machine with wires attached to both children. Showing a reading of their heart and a stand beside each machine that had glucose bag hooked onto it with a line leading to a cannula that had been inserted into the both children's hands. The other side of the beds was bedside cabinets. A jug of water and plastic cup on a tray. Resting on top of each bedside cabinet and two chairs placed at the side of the eldest girl bed next to the bedside cabinet. On the left was a wash basin and different sizes, disposable gloves. Just beside the door. Underneath the window was three bins containing different colour bags with labels attached to each bin. The rubbish bin had a black bag in. The hazard bin had a yellow bag in and the laundry bin had a red bag in. Opposite the wash basin on the over side of the room was a stainless steel trolly. that had a medical cabinet with a lock containing first aid equipment. Next to the trolly was two bed tables and another door that entered a small bathroom. Containing a toilet, sink and a walk-in show.

The eldest child hat long curly mousse brown hair. That came down to the shoulders. brown eyes and a button nose, with rosy cheeks. She was skinny and slightly short for her age.

The youngers child had fine blond short hair, blue eyes and a chubby face. Puffed out rosy cheeks and was average size for her age.

They both had hospital grown on, with hospital bedding pulled up to the arms pits. They had both their arms on the outside of the covers. A pulse oximetry placed onto the left hand finger of each girl. The wiring was attached to the chest on both girls and the youngers girl had an oxygen mask on layed down. The empty plates and cups show the children had just finished eating and drinking. The eldest girl was sat up in bed resting against the pillows.

As the doctor left the room she pulled open the blinds so the outside was able to view in. shutting the door behind her. The doctor stood watching from the other side. Detective 'O' Brien sat on the chair nearest to the eldest girls with her notebook open as she began the interview. Writing down everything that was said. The Social Worker sat next to detective 'O' Brien. With her A4 pad also jogging down as she listens to the interview.

"My name is detective 'O' Brien. I'm here today just to ask you a few question on the case that I am dealing with. You aren't in any trouble and as you don't have an adult with you at this present time. Mrs Bagshaw from Child Social Services is here as a liaison to represent you as an adult. Also she will be helping you to find a family member or a family to take care of you and your sister. Till you both are old enough to live on your own. Please can you state your name, age for me?".

The girl spoke very quietly was a slight croak in her voice.

"My name is Summer Mroczkowska. I'm eleven years old".

"Can I ask you your sister name and age as she too young to speak?".

"Yes, Autumn Mroczkowska. She two years old".

"Can you remember anything that happened earlier?".

"No, I only remember I went to bed and then waking up heard feeling sick and a bad headache. Nothing else.".

"That ok, do you know what time you went to bed and fell asleep?".

"It was around six. I played on my tablet in bed and went asleep about seven".

"Did you hear anything unusual during the time you were playing on your tablet?".

"No, only my mum tv and when she was walking about down stairs".

"Do you Know what has happened?".

"No, is my mum here".

"No, I have some bad news. Early on you mum was a victim of crime. She had been murder and was announced dead on arrival. You and your sister was knocked out with a chemical solution. So you and your sister was rushed into hospital. Where you and your sister was given medical treatment. Are you understanding what I am saying?".

With tears streaming down her eyes. Dripping onto the sheet. The Social Care Worker grabbed a tissue out of her bag and handed it to the girl. As she scrunches the tissue up in her hand. Rubbing it along the bottom of her eyes.

"Yes, I understand. My mum is dead".

"I know this is very upsetting for you. Would you like me to give you a couple of minutes before carrying on with the interview?".

"No, I am ok. It just I couldn't help myself from crying. knowing that my mum has left me and never got to say goodbye".

"Do you know your father, where he lives and if he still alive?".

"Only what my mum told me. I never met him so I don't know if he still alive or where he lives."

"Can you give me his name?".

"Sorry I can't remember".

"That fine, is there anyone you know?".

"Yes nana and grandpa. I have an uncle and aunties awell".

"Can you tell me where they live?".

"Somewhere in Grimsby. My mum did keep a contact number and address in her phone book".

"Where did she keep it?".

"On her, in her handbag".

"Do you know where she keeps the handbag. when she at home?".

"Yes, in her bedroom. She hangs it on the coat hanger on the back of the door".

"Thank you Summer, that be all for now. If you think of anything else give us a call at the police station. It was nice meeting you. I let you rest now".

Detective 'O' Brien stood up and headed out of the door followed by the Social Care Worker. Headed for the reception area to speak to Dr Soloman. Before headed back to the police station. Then saying her bye to the doctor and the Social Care work. As she headed out of the hospital.

Chapter Twelve

THE CLUES

Detetive Jones finished off his reported on the case. While professor Wilkinson and Dr Harpe sorted out the evidents ready for the meeting that was arranged later in the day. As the sun shined throught the window. The beem blinded out the screen of the computer. So detective Jones pulled down the blinds and switch on the light. Picking up his cup. Slurping the cold coffee that had been sitting there for sometime. Tipping the chair slightly, before leaning forward and pressing the left side of the mouse to save the file. Has he stands up to head for the printer to retrieve the copys of the case work. He had done, the phone rang.

"Detective Jones office".

A deep man's voice came over the receiver.

"Detective Jones I'm calling about your car. We had finger prints taken and found nothing".

"Right, so I can pick it up then".

"No, not at the moment we just got to finish sorting a few bits on the vehicle. Before releasing the car back to you".

"What time will the car be ready".

"Three 'o' clock today. So if you come in about two forty five. I get the paper work done. As we need a couple of signatures from you".

"Ok, see you then. Bye".

Detective Jones places back the receiver and collects the paperwork. Placing it into a brown folder. Before he entires his office. Detective Jones glimpse through the glass of the door of detective 'O' Brien office. Noticing she was still typing away. Not even noticing detective Jones as he paused for a split-second. Placing the file into the cabinet and then heading to the chief inspector's office with the other copy of the same report. He walked into the secretary office that had a door leading into the chief inspector's office. Where a middle age women sat behind a desk. With a computer, phone and an intercom.

"You are looking lovely today, Heather".

Heather was in her early forties. Slim built and just below five foot. She had blue eyes with black hair that came down passed her shoulders. Halfway down her back. her cheek bone puffed out. Making her face tiny and round. With red lipstick on her lips. Freckles that ran around her forehead, down to her cheeks. The short sleeve blue dress button from top to bottom. Had a white lace collar. Her hands were tiny with a ring or two on each index finger. Somewhere gold and others where silver. With a thin gold neckless that hung around her neck. Her shoes where pointy and beige, with thick soles.

"Thank you for your compliment detective Jones. What can I do for you on this fine day".

"I have the report for your boss, need to see him".

"Just take a seat and I see if he is free to see you".

While detective Jones sat down. The secretary pressed the button on the intercom and waited for an answer from the chief inspector Karl.

"Yes Heather".

"Sir, we have detective Jones here. He got the report and would like to speak to you".

"Ok, Heather I need you just to pop in for a minute. Before sending detective Jones in. As I have an urgent letter that I need you to type up for me. So I can sign and have you post it before the day is out. That be all".

Heather stood up and enter the chief inspector's officer. Holding an A4 pad with a biro placed in the loop of the pad that held the pages together. The secretary was in the office for some time. A good fifteen minutes before coming out and given detective Jones the ok, to go in.

The office bent around a corner. Opening out into a large room with a door at the back. Behind the desk. That entred into a toilet and wash facilities. The desk was mahogany. With a reddish leather top. Held by metal rivets and curved out legs. That curved slightly at the top for design. The chair that the chief inspector was sat on was the same design as the desk. On the other side was two leather chair. A computer sat on the left. On the right was a phone with an intercom linked into it. On the right side of the room that took most of the wall up. Was a large bookcase that was only half filled with new and old books. Some of the empty bookcase shelves had ornaments. Sat there gathering dust on top of them. Next to the door behind the desk was medium size painting with mahogany frame. That came out two inches and went all the way round. On the left was a large window. Separated into several plain sheets of glass. Light beige binds that hanged on each side of the window. With two strings. One to turn and the other to draw the blinds together. A dark red thick carpet. that the furniture sunk into it. In the middle of the room was two dark red leather settees. with metal rivets running around the arms and back of the settees. Just between the settees was a glass coffee table. Where a black marble figure of a woman as the legs. Holding an oval piece of glass to finish off the design of the coffee table. At the back of the wall that go into a bend. Rest a fifty-inch flat screen tv.

As detective Jones sat opposite the chief inspector Karl. The secretary came back in holdind an silver tray. Containing a sliver coffee pot, sliver jug of milk and two small stainless steel pots with suger and sweetener. With two white cups, face down onto white saucers and a plate with different biscuit layed nicely out. Placing the tray down onto the desk, leaving the room.

As the chief inspector began to speak.

"Coffee detective Jones".

"Yes, please".

"White, three sugars".

"You remembered".

"I like an elephant, I never forget. What you do need to talk about then, biscuit".

"Thank you sir, I never say no. I'm worried, about this person".

"Well I can't read your mind, spit it out. Which person".

"The murderer Sir. They know everything about me. I don't know if I can carry on with the case sir".

"Look get some backbone. Obviously the person knows you. You not in any danger. The murderer is just using you. Don't let it get to you. You are like a son to me. This time next year you be sitting in this chair I'm sat on. Looking back on this case and feeling proud of yourself".

"Your right sir".

"Cause I am right. I read your report and let you know what I think. Now get back to work and get this son of a bitch strung up by their nuts. So we can celebrate with a few pints down at the local".

"Yes, sir".

"I hear you tied a knot in it. That there is married bells. Get my drift".

"How do you know that sir".

"The walls talk, it amazing what you hear".

"Yes sir, after the case".

"Well, next time don't do it on my time ok. I speak to you later".

"Yes sir, I won't do it again".

As detective Jones left the office. Checking the time. He decided to pop for lunch and a swift drinks before picking his vehicle up from the garage. Grabbing a pack of peppermint and cigarettes from the shop so he could cover up the smell of booze. Walking into the garage office that had a contact with the police. Where the investigators use the garage for doing their fingerprints on vehicle. Standing next to the counter. Waiting for the mechanic as he bangs the top of metal round bell. An average guy walks through the door on the other side of the counter.

The mechanic was just under six foot. Chubby face with a very short dark hair. Brown eyes and stubble, from not shaving. Gold earings and a thick gold chain. Wearing a grey jumpsuit with a sewn in label. That had the name of the company. Both sleeves were rolled up. Showing tatoos down both arms and across the left hand knuckles. You could see tatoo's just below the neck. Where the top button was undone. The stomach part flaped over. Causing the jumpsuit button to just keep the jumpsuit together. Laced up brown boots. Tucked underneath the legs of the jumpsuit.

The office was an odd long shaped room. With a counter going from one side of the room to the other side. With a door, where the top of the counter life up and a door opens inwards. This half the room. making one side the customers and the other side the staffs. On the customer side was a venue machine that did hot and cold drinks and another venue machine. Opposite the drinks machine was a snack machine that did chocolate bars and sweets. The floor was tiled with the colour of grey and the walls was painted dark green. The ceiling was white with yellowish stains.

"Yes".

"Detective Jones, come to pick up my vehical".

"Got identification Mr Jones".

Pulling out his wallet and placing the identification onto the counter. As the man picks it up the card. Looking back and forward a couple of times at the picture on the card. Then at detective Jones. Before he handed it back to the detective Jones. Then pulling out from underneath the counter. Documents, as he flipped through the pages putting a cross where detective Jones needed to sign.

"Your vehical be ready soon Mr Jones. Just need three signatures from you. One for your house, one for everthing you own and one for all your money".

"Trying to be funny mate".

"I take it you are not that type of guy. I was only trying to break the ice mate. I take it you take life too serious".

"No, just not in that kind of mood today. I have a lot on my plate".

"Understand Mr Jones. I have a shoulder if you would like to spill the beans and have a little cry about whatever bothering you. It will lift a lot of your mind. Trust me you fill hundred times better".

"I think I'll give that one a miss, if you don't mind".

"Ok Mr Jones. Sign these than just take a seat over their and I bring your vehicle around when I am done".

Detective Jones signed the documents and sat waiting to pick up is vehicle. As he pulled up in the police station car park. Detective Jones sat there in his car with the engine still running for a while. Thinking about everything that as happened this past week. Before noticing that it was nearly time to brief the officers. While waiting for detective Jones to start. The room was filled with noise from everyone chatting. With a sudden quietness. when detective Jones walk in the room. You could hear a pin drop. As they fixed their eyes onto him. Watching detective Jones walk up to the whiteboard containing the evidence and as he spoke out.

"Good afternoon everyone. It comes to my attention that we all failed. This is not good enough and I am not happy that the mother of them poor children. Never had a chance to be saved. Very sad, so very sad this has happened. Two days we had and what did we have to show for it, nothing!. What are we a bunch of idiots, no!. You all need to pull your socks up and start putting hundred and ten percent into this case. As I want results. I not going to keep banging on about it. Time running out and we need to bang a nail into the nuts of this scum and stop the person before they strike again. Professor willincole I let you start. What do have?".

"Well I been studying the evidence we have so far. Which I have come up with some pointers that might lead us to solve this case. The first thing I like to mention. The murderer has sexual outburst over the victims eyes. This is why they like to watch as the victims die and the second thing is the murderer likes to keep the victims alive long enough. So the womb they remove is fresh. That makes me believe this person must eat the womb on the same night of the murder. So the womb doesn't lose the taste they hunger for. Another thing is the murderer has mention. That they had a bad childhood.

Making them to resent their mother. Causing the murderer to build up pain and anger inside them. To release the pain and anger. The murderer is relating the victims to be like their mother and by taking their life making this person feel relieved from the pain and anger. That only go away for a day or so. Coming back with vengeance. This now brings me to the eight clues. That I have underlined. We are looking for a woman driver. So the first clue will be a biggish car. Somewhere along the lines of a four seater. Maybe a six-setter car. The car will properly have teddys resting on the back window. With a child aboard sign stuck to the glass of the back window. It be tidy, just a dirty floor from being deprived of a hoovering. Second clue is the woman as a family of two, also married. Three clue is she works long hours. During the day by started in the morning and finishing late afternoon. Four clue is the time. Given the time of year it get dark around seven. This gives us a time when it will happen. Estimated between seven and seven thirty pm. Five clue is the murderer will break into the vehicle before that time. Waiting for the women to leave work and get into the vehicle. Six clue is the woman will enter the car and the murderer will grab her from behind. Knocking her out and tiring her up. Moving her to the passager seat before the murderer drives the vehicle to the destination. This brings me to the seven clue. The destination, we looking for a car park in the Grimsby area. I don't think it the hospital car park. It more likely to be an empty deserted car park in a quiet area. Pub, doctor's surgery, church or school's car park. Somewhere not far from the area where the woman works. Ten to fifteen minutes away. The last clue is the time the murderer will murder the women. I say it be more properly eight pm. This brings me to the end. I like to pass you over to my colleague Dr Harpe".

"I like to start off with the feeling the murderer as mention in their letter. It please me to know that the murderer is opening up and reaching out. It like the murderer wants closer on their childhood. By not talking verbally to us. By writing the feeling of hurt, pain and sadness that built up over the years. That made the person withdraw from the world, with anger and rage. Medical terms, by the murderer keeping everything locked inside for many years and not seeking help. Causing the person to snap. Mainly producing unknown schizophrenic that is an illness like schizophrenia. The reason for this is that when a person as a mental illness and the doctors are unable to diagnose the illness. It will be recorded as unknown. I believe the murderer doesn't sleep too well. By having nightmares of their past. This is common. It's a trauma known as a shock to the brain. Causing the memorys to repeat. While the person body is relaxed sleeping the cortex plays the trauma. Making the brain think it real. Sending signals to every nerve within the body. This can cause the body to sweat and heart rate to speed up. Making the body flinch and move about. The brain will automatically wake the person up to pervent any damage to the organs. Mainly the heart. As the heart beats rapidly it can cause blood pressure to rise, lack of oxygen due to not enough oxygen getting into the blood. That is being pumped around the body at a fast rate. Which prevent the brain from getting the oxygen it needs from the cell of the blood. That enters the brain. The murderer feels they have a connection with detective Jones. Wanting to open up as a friend. They feel comfortable connecting, trusting and feeling safe. Knowing that they have that person in their life that they are able to relieve their worries and confession that eat away their inside. The murderer like to joke. Using the bald patch of detective Jones hair. Feeling sexually aroused when the murderer looks into the eyes of the victims. To the point of ejaculation. As you can see the murderer base their letter around riddles. They do this for a reason. It not just the eight clues in the letter or the victims they are going to attack in the next couple of day. It a game for the murderer that they like to play and find it fascinating that they draw attention to their self. This is most common in a person who is suffering from mental illness. As they will need to draw attention. Known as attention seeking. This is most command in children when they want the attention of their parent. by playing up. Causing trouble and sometimes lashing out at their parent. The same thing happening here. The murderer is lashing out for the attention. They do this by playing a game and taking the victim life. This person may of not got the attention when they were younger. That cause them to feel lonely, shy and scared. To put this to term. They may have spent a lot of time in their own space making up invisible friend. When attending school they would have sat by their self and play by their self. Finding it hard to make friends because of being shy around others. They would have been scared a lot. Especially at school. Causing them to be bullied a lot. I believe this could of been girls that bullied the person. Causing the person to attack female later on in life. These are some of the things that could be the start of the trigger. The meaning to this is that the person could of crossed one of these paths later on in their life that triggered. The impulse in their brains causing them to attack their victims. Changing the way the person thinks. Making them believe that they are doing right by it and taking away the memories of the past. Just for that period of time the person feels normal again. Something may have happened during the first victim. That may have caused the murderer to eat the organ. Causing them to become audited to the taste of the organ. Even known the murderer took it has a reminder of every victim they murdered. It still was taken from the victim for a certain reason. This was to take away the childbirth from a women. The murderer may have a lot more victims that we don't know about. Hidden away for ever. Never to be found again. This brings me to the end for now. Ho how I love to get into the mind of this person. Just to see how they're brain tick. It interest's me to know that the mind of this person is so educational in way's you would never know".

"Thank you Dr Harpe for that weird ending. You sick mother fucker. Look I may be the detective in charge of the investigation but can't stand here listen to you getting a hard on by thinking about murderer brian. This is me, I'm a total wanker and I always will be this way. Now I like to pass you on to Kelly, my star pupil. The only one who manage to change my mind on psychic, so Kelly it over to you".

As she sat there and placed both palms onto the table six inches apart from each other. She took a couple of deep breaths before she began.

"I see a dark area with tree surrounding the area. They swing from side to side. A gentle wind blows, not too cold. There a moonlight in the background that shines off the clouds in the sky. Given different shades of colour. Blue, black and white within the sky. Lamp shade light up the area. Like a reddish orange. I see it now, it a car park but empty. No a silver seven seat car rest on the north. Just underneath a tree branch. Number three come into my head. What you saying. Yes, the number three is, is the bay. It the third car park space on the north side of the car park. There a sound in the background. What is it. I'mm let me think, got it. The sound I hear is traffic, lots of traffic. Means the car park is situated near the main road, busy main road. I now focusing on the car. I see two dark figure. Can't make out the identity, man or woman. No no, I see the blade, a silver blade. So much red everywhere. Wait what this. Ho no, no, no!, the figure had pulled something out and holding it in their hand. The hand has a blue plastic glove. But they wearing something else underneath the glove. I can't make out what it is maybe another glove of some sort. It can't be, it is I can see the blood dripping from it. The fresh of the human organ, clung between the person's fingers. Nothing else, I can't see anymore. Why won't you show me anymore. Why ho why".

At this point kelly head drops forward. With her eyes shut. still sat upright. With her palms remain in the same place.

Then detective Jones finished up with the last speech.

"Thank you for that Kelly. That all for now, let get to work".

Chapter Thirteen

THE CAR PARK

The day had arrived upon us. As the sky started to darken with the night turning mild. A young woman leaves her place of work. She walks over to her vehicle that was parked between the car and van. Just on the opposite side of the road. She stood looking for the car keys, in her handbag. That was hidden, between the purse and makeup bag. Just at the bottom of her handbag. As she grabs hold of the keys. Pulling them out of the handbag. Causing the purse to drop out of the handbag and spill all the purse contents over the floor. near the driver sided of the vehicle. She bent down to pick up the purse and contents that had split out. Not realizing the woman had missed a few coins that rolled under the vehicle. Placing the purse into her handbag and putting the key into the keyhole of the vehicle door. She opens the door throwing her handbag onto the passager side seat. Clicking the seat belt into places as she sits behind the steering wheel of her vehicle. Before intercepting the key into the ignition and turning it to start the engine. As the engine was still running. The woman grabs hold of the mirror with both hands and turning it so she was able to run her fingers through her hair before she decided to drive off. While the woman sat there looking into the little mirror. Flicking her hair back. She notices a figure in the background. Hidden behind the drivers seat. Causing her to be startled. Before she was able to do anything a hand came around her. Locking around her throat with the other hand covering her face with a rag. That released some sort of chemical substance. While the woman struggled to break free. She started to feel light headed. Before everything went blank.

The woman was a short person with long straight brown hair tied back into a ponytail. That came down past her shoulders. She had a white furry hair band holding the ponytail into place. With a couple of hair clips on both sides of the hair. Her eyes were brown with long eyelashes, darken by black eye mascara. The cheek bones were puffed out and a small rounded face. She had two gold earring studs. One in each ear containing light purple stones and she was well spoken. The woman was medium built. Wearing her work uniform. That was navy blue with white lining around the sleeves and collier. With metal buttons that clip together. The woman had a belly button piercing hidden underneath the uniform. Black trouser which was neatly pressed. That ran down the centre of both trouser legs. On her left arm was a gold bangle. A wedding ring with a diamond stone on her index finger. The shoe was black slip-on, with thin soles. Where you could see multicolored shocks slightly between the tongue of the slip-on and bottom of her trouser's.

As the person got out of the vehicle and open the drivers door. Wearing a black cotton hat, jacket, trousers and shoes which contained silver within them. Moving the woman who was out cold and was now slouch over on the driver seat. With her head leaning towards her handbag. Dragging the woman body out of the vehicle and onto the back seat of the vehicle. Laying her down on to her back across the seat. The murderer then pulls out the toolbox that they had placed in the vehicle early. When the murderer picked locked to the vehicle door without anyone noticing. As the murderer open the tool box pulling out the item required. Then shutting the toolbox and shoving the toolbox between the back seat and the driver seat. Tying up the woman's arms and legs with rope. Stuffing one rag into her mouth and using another rag to tie it around her head so it covers the mouth. Closing the back door. The murderer got into the driver's seat.

Pulling out their compact disc from their top pocket of the jacket. Placing it into the CD player. Pressing play and then drove the car to the area. The person planned to take the woman life. As the person park the car in the graveyard car park by the church. Next to a tree that was leaning over slightly with the branched leaves inches away from the roof of the car. The sound of vehicle in the background from the main road and with the leafs blowing in the wind on this mild night. Was dimmed out by the music from the stereo system in the car as the person open the car door. Closing it and then opening the back door. The murderer pulled the woman out of the car. Laying her body onto the cold car park floor. Sitting on the back seat with their legs out of the car watching the woman as the murderer waited for her to awake from her deep sleep. Thirty minutes had passed and the woman began to open her eyes. With everything blurred at first. Feeling that her head was about to exposed, confused and scared with everything happen around her. Noticing her surrounding when the woman sight came back to her. As she began to realizing that she was unable to defend herself and felt paralyse from not been able to move her legs and arms. The murderer kneels down beside the woman in a sitting upright position. While they spoke out to the helpless victim laying there shivering.

"Hello there, don't be scared my love. Everything going to be fine, trust me. I know there will be pain. Only for a little while. So it all be over very soon. Then you be able to rest in peace. I going to tell you a little story. So shh and listen very carefully. I gave the police a few clues to work out. But obviously I think they all haven't got an ounce of brain between them. I bet you they sit there drinking their coffee. Talking about shit that happen in their life. Instead of doing their jobs. Then they wonder why crime rate has gone up. What a wasted of space and taxpayers money. I say bomb the lot of them. That should save time and money in the long future. Not even one clue, lead or even coming close to stopping me. Well what can I say. Utterly total wankers called themselves police officers. Pigs that what they are. Just a load of idiots who are not doing their job properly. This is what I mean. Your in this dilemma because they just don't give a toss about you. Basically you mean nothing to them. Not even your life. So sad, I bet you feel like nothing, knowing that. They scum, how could they. Like I care, not!. No, no I just here to take your life away and get what I came for. You are properly thinking you evil heartless bastard. I would agree with you. One hundred percent I am definite that type person. I tell you why I do the things I do. It all about what happened to me in my life. All through my life I had been ill-treated, bullied and took advantage of. Then one day came. Just like a click in the head. I bet you wondering what the chick was in my head. I getting there and I going tell you exactly about it. The click was a wake-up call. That change my life in so many ways. From being a total loser to someone who can stand on their own feet. Then that day came. I said to myself no mother fuckers will walk over me again. You must know this, life a bitch. It will creep up on you and bit you in the ass. One way or another. It doesn't matter who you are in life or where you come from, it will always creep up on you when your not expecting it. You properly saying to yourself why me?. Why you that a very good question. I tell you why you were the chosen one. For two days I studied you ingrate lenght. As I like to get to know my victims. To become acquaintances with them. This is what I know about your pittance life, a mother of two young children. Lovely little things they are. They just don't have any understanding of danger in life and don't worry your children are in no harm. Children are not my kind of scene. If you get my drifted. Only interested in youngish woman. For the suffering that so call, don't even want to say her name. Must I, very well then. My mother, if you can call her that. Getting back to you, married to you husband. I must say he a very nice person to talk to. We kind of crossed paths in the cafe this morning and we had a good chat. Don't worry not interested in him. So you always know that your children will always have one parent in their life. Person who works with the elderly, how nice. One thing is that you are a sinner like any other woman that walks this earth. Mean that you have to pay for them sins. I will tell you that the pain will be horrendous, not to worry. It will only last as long as you fright it. So my best answer to this is let me get what I want and give up. It will free you of the pain. Leaving your love ones with the memories. Do you have any last words, maybe confession that you might need to get off your chest. Scream and I will cut your tongue out, believe me!. I don't mess around".

At this point the murderer lent over. Pulling down the rag and removing the other rag from her month. So the woman could speak. Even know she was scare she put on a brave face on. By not pleading for her life. To ask the murderer a question.

"What is your name?".

"My name, O I like you. No one as ever asked my name before. I had please don't kill me, go to fucking hell and your not worth a piece of shit on my shoe. Never my name, the Scalp Slayer that my name".

"Yes, I heard about you on the news and in the papers".

"How wonderful. I even bet they told or written bad things about me".

"Yes, they say you are a very dangerous person. Who murders young woman. That we should stay away. Call the police immediately".

"So true, I am that type of person. It's a bit late for you to try and stay away figure of speech. Do you think I am that type of person?. You can tell me the truth I won't bit. I promise, I a big softy in some ways".

"I don't think you that type of person. Deep down there some humanity there. That part is true and you have a problem, that for sure. You do know there help out there. As not every woman is like your mother. They will listen to you and treated your condition. So you be able to live a normal life".

"Normal life!, too late for me. Very true, I may say so. You have an interesting point. I take that into account. I sure there that one boring person who will sit a listen to my shit life story. It may even be fun. But you have to know I came here and pick you for a reason. You will die. Does that scare you?".

"Yes it does, it scares me a lot. I need to ask you something. Can't you loosen these ropes a bit. I think my blood not circulating in my hands and feet. I can feel pins and needles all over. I won't escape, I promised".

"Ok, try to escape. It will be the last thing you do".

As the murderer untied the ropes on the woman legs and then arms. She knees the murderer in the stomach and pushes the person over. Getting up to run the murderer jumps forward and grabs her leg cause her to fall to the ground. With the blood gushing from her eyebrow. Has the murderer pulls her back onto the ground retiring her arms and legs. The woman struggles to get loose. Gagging the woman mouth. Placing their arm over the woman neck. Pressing down slightly and making her unable to breathe properly. On the verge of passing out. The murderer placed their face inches away from the woman face. While speaking to her.

"You silly woman, think you can escape from me. You really think I am that stupid. Well you have me all wrong. I thought you was an understanding person. How I got it wrong. I really trusted you and you just like anyone else. Took advantage of my good will. For this I will make you suffer in ways, you never think of".

As the person pulls out the surgical knife. Using the pointed end. They stick it into the knuckle of the hand. Twisting it around. Causing tears to run down the side of the woman face. Has the murderer carried on with what they had to say.

"Now listen to me, listen very carefully. I don't blame for trying to escape. I would have done the same. So we start again, clean slate. I will be opening you up. To obtain the meat that I require. You will be awake during the procedure. After I finished with your dead corpse I will take that head of hair off and shove it into a box for that detective Jones in charge of this murder case. Then I leave your rotten corpse to lay here in the gutter. For everyone to see. Understand this, I could of made it easy for you. But you brought it upon yourself to make this so much harder than it is. Well is that the time, we don't want to be late now. I think the times come, to say goodbye".

Has the murderer removes the knife from the woman knuckles. They pull open the top of the woman uniform. Revealing her belly button with a butterfly ring. That had a silver bar with the butterfly at the top and colours of red and blue within it. At the bottom was a ball with a blue stone in the centre that reflected light from the street lights. That lit the car park. Using the sharp pointed end of the knife. The murderer pierced the woman skin just below the belly button. While the blood runs out over the sides of the open wound. The murderer uses their index fingers to widen the wound enough. To remove the stomach contents. So they were able to get to the organ that the murderer needed to cut and remove. The pain ran straight through the woman body causing her whole body stiffened. While tear ran down her face and screaming out in pain. Muffled by the rags that were stuffed in and tied around her head. Before everything went blank from the pain. While her body laid there in shock slowly shutting down. One by one each organ closed down till the last organ. The heart as the beats slowly faded away. During this time, the murderer had removed the meat that they required. Placing the stomach contented that had spilt out over the sides of the woman body. Pushing it back into the stomach and closing the wound enough to prevent the content of the stomach spilling back out and to nicely stayed in. Only showing very little through the gaps of the wound. Then clicking the uniform button's back together. The murderer grabbed the serrated knife. Moving the woman body to a sitting up position. With her head resting against the vehicle door. The murderer saws into the skin and hair with the serrated knife. Removing the skin and hair from the top of the woman scalp while the blood ran down the side of her face and the reddish liquid brain fluid seeped from the right ear. Dripping onto the shoulder of the woman uniform. Laying the woman's body back down onto the cold car park floor. The murderer places everything they had taken into the toolbox. Leaving her and the vehicle as the murderer walk away into the dark mild night.

Chapter Fourteen

VICTIM THREE

As daybreak comes the thick fog fills the sky with mist. Making the air cold and the surrounding hard to see. A daybreak entries the car park with the fog light beaming through the thick fog. Father Joe step out of the vehicle to investigate the person by the car. Thinking it was another drunk who had fallen asleep. As he got closer. Father Joe couldn't believe what he had seen. Standing in complete shock. He slowly steps backwards till his back pressed against his vehical. Blending down into the vehicle while still facing the murdered victim. Father Joe open the glove department just below the steering wheel. Grading the mobile phone. Dialing the emergency number.

Father Joe was a short, skinny man. He had fine brown hair with specks of grey all over his hair. That only grow around the sides. Which father Joe flick the hair from the right side. Over his bald patch. The eyes were ice blue and his skin was frail with the colour of pale. that the wrinkles never disappeared in his face. He Had an odd long face that the skin sucked in at the cheeks. Causing the cheek bones to form shape in the skin. Making father Joe chin long and narrow rounded. Wearing a black top and trousers. The top had a white collier folded underneath the top collier appearing through the gap of the top. Father Joe had black shiny shoes, with black laces tired into bows.

As a young lady speaks over the mobile, on the other side. The sweat from father Joe face formed a ring around part of the mobile that was press against the ear. Which happen a lot when he was nerves. Still in shock father Joe managed to still hold it together while answering to the call.

"Emergency services, which service would you like. Police, ambulances or fire brigade".

"Can I have the police please".

"Hold on just putting you through now".

While father Joe waited for an answer on the other end. Standing by his vehicle. As the ringing tone came from the other line before a person answer on the other end.

"Police, how can I help".

"This is father Joe. I arrived at my church in the graveyard just off the main road opposite the Grimsby hospital for a service today and come across a young woman I believe has been murder".

"Can I ask where abouts you found the young lady".

"I found her in the car park. Outside the chapel of rest. Perched up against the park vehicle. With her body laid on the ground and her head that is missing hair at the top. Resting against the vehicle door".

"Ok sir, we have officers on the way to you. Stay where you are as we need to get a statement from you".

After father Joe ended the call he got back into the vehicle closing the door and waited for the police to turn up. He listens to the music in the vehicle to take his mind of the young woman. Detective Jones was in the main investigation room with some of the staff. Working on the case. Trying to understand was they went wrong on the last set of clues given to them by the murderer and why they didn't catch the murderer before the time ran out. At this point, everyone in the room were tired. With a few of them, that had fallen asleep. While detective Jones sat in the chair swing from side to side. Tapping the pen against his lip looking at the evident around the white board. As the door open an officer entered the room. Walking up to the detective Jones. He made eye contact with the officer. With the pen now resting against his bottom lip.

"Sorry to bother you, sir. They found another body at the old church in the graveyard. The caller was father Joe. He waiting there to give a statement".

"Thanks, officer Blog. How you and your family".

Officer Blog was a thin seven-foot guy. He always bang his head when entering rooms as the door frames were too low. making him, have to duck everytime. The hair was dark brown, short and parted. Beginning to fade away at the top. His eyebrows were bushy and his face was thin with the exception of the cheeks that puffed out.

"Fine sir, oh congratulation on your big day sir".

"Well new travels very fast around here these days, thank you anyway".

Detective Jones stood up. Placing the pen onto the desk that was behind him. Turning around facing the officers.

"Right boys and girls. I've just been informed the person we were looking to save last night has been found. Professor Willincole and Dr Harpe you're with me. Detective 'O' Brein I need you to keep charged in here. The rest of you lot. Get yourself a coffee, wake yourself up as when I get back. I am sending everyone home for a few hour to rest. Ready for the next clues that come in. From the murderer. In the meantime, I need those reports on my desk. As chief inspector Karl not going to be a happy bunny and most properly going to rip my head off. Put it where the sun don't shine".

While detective Jones left with the professor Willincole and the Dr Harpe, the other sat getting their reports ready for detective Jones when he got back. Father Joe looked up into the center mirror that had a sunshine air freshener hanging off it. With flashing blue light in the background. Detective Jones taps against father Joe window. As he opens the vehical door to speak to the detective. The professor Willincole and Dr Harpe went off. To do there own thing. Walking around the vehical with the victim laying against it. Discussing and pointing out things they believe to be evidents. Without destroying the crime scene.

"Father Joe can you step out of the vehicle please".

As father Joe step out and stood face detective Jones who was now pointing his index finger towards the vehicle with flashing blue lights.

"I like you to sit in the back of the vehicle father Joe so I can get a statement of you".

Detective Jones shut the back door of the vehicle on the drive's side. Walking around to the other side to get into the front. He pulls the handle of the vehicle and opens the door. At the same time, the crime scene investigator parks up next to the vehicle. She steps out walking around to the back of the vans opening the doors. While speaking to the detective Jones.

"Hi, sexy, how my lover doing today. Still coming around tonight, I've got your favorite meal and you so going to love the dessert".

"Yep, I'll be there. Might be bit late. You know, got to go and see chief inspector Karl. Believe me, the shit really hit the fan. I blow it this time. Fucked up and still no further catching the murderer".

"We talk later about that love. Your doing your best. The chief inspector Karl got to understand that, at least".

"I wish, he a good guy. But the guy got a nasty bite to him. When he blow his top. He like a bull in a china shop. Scare the shit out of me".

"Just let it go through one ear and out the other".

"Thanks for listening babe, you alway seem to make things better".

"Don't worry about it, love. Don't let it get to you. It just a job at the end of the day. That all it is".

"I know babe, I know. I try to get through it. Maybe there light around the corner and all this is just one bad dream. I going to wake up and there before my eye's. I have the son of a bitch locked up in the cell. Before they murder another young woman. That doesn't know they the next victim".

"I just say this before I get to work, chin-up, be positive and you will nail the person. One of these days. They going to make a big mistake that will lead you to them. Ok love, we talk later about this over dinner. Member I am here for you. Your problems are my problem and we work at them together".

At that point, Sophia went one way and the detective got into the vehicle closing the door behind him and started the interview with father Joe.

"My name is detective Jones and father Joe I would like you to start from the beginning and tell me everything about today. I'll need times on everything".

"Well, detective Jones. I got into my car at eight this morning and came straight here. Didn't stop for petal or anything. Just came straight from home. Only packing the bible's, booklet of the service today and song book in the boot of my car. As I like to get here early. A couple of hours early. Before the service, so I can have the chapel of rest ready".

"What time did you arrive here".

"It takes me about an hour from my home address. Pending on the traffic or if I needed to make a stop. It would of been about nine".

"Home address".

"I live in louth, with my wife and two children that are all grow up. But won't leave the birds nest. I pass you my card, it as my home address and number on it".

Passing detective Jones a small card with a fancy printout of his home address and home number on it. Detective Jones placed it into his coat pocket and carried on.

"How old are you father Joe".

"Seventy-five, I be seventy-six next month".

"Really seventy-five, you don't look it. Anyway carry on".

"I pulled up, noticing the person laying there on the fall. It was hard to see. As the fog blinded my vision. The first reaction I had was, a drunk that had passed out. It's happens a lot. There been a few times I had people sleeping around here from drinking too much. So I decided to get out of my car, wake them up. Then to my surprise. When I got close enough. I got the biggest shock of my life. It was like my heart was beating to a dozen. I just felt sick inside, seeing that poor young woman laying there. The poor thing, no one should every have to go through that. I'll be lighting a candle for her. Maybe special Sunday service for her. Now where was I, that right. It just knocked me off my feet, look!. My hand are still shaking from it".

Holding his hand out straight for detective Jones to see. Then placing it down back onto his lap. While the detective glance at the notebook. Thinking of the next question to ask.

"Tell me father Joe did you touch anything, move the body. Maybe step on anything by accident, when you were close to the victim".

"No, all I did was step backwards till I reached my car. Then I took my mobile out of the glove department on the drive's side".

"So you call us straight away".

"Yes, I believe so".

"Thank you father Joe. That be all for now. I'll be in touch if there anything else I need to know. I advise you to contact the people who are having service and tell them that the service will be delayed for one day. Due to unforeseen-circumstances. Have a good day father Joe".

Father Joe got into his vehicle. While detective Jones walked up to Sophia. To get the outcome of the crime scene and any new evidents that could bring the murderer to justice.

"Sophia what do we have then".

"Well, detective Jones. She was kill in the same way. This means that it was the same person who murdered the other victims".

"Is there any new evidence. That could help with the case".

"Just some item on the victim. Name of victim Rebecca Robinson, address, age mid-twenties and the vehicle the victim laid against is her. I have the vehicle sent to the garage to be striped and check over for any samples that can be tested for DNA".

"Ok, thank Sophia. I see you later".

He walks away, turning toward the direction the professor Willincole and Dr Harpe was standing. Still discussing their views on the crime scene.

"Hello, boys. Professor Willincole what's your views on this".

"I come up with a number of pointers, first one. I was looking at the victim. Notices on her clothes there was dirty wet patches in several places. Now I know there's dirt on the floor and obviously, the victims will have dirt patches. But as you can see. The patches are on the front and back of the victim's clothes. The second one was the eyebrow. It has been split open. Well if you put two and two together. The answer will revive itself. This what I come up with. Somehow the victim managed to break free, tried to escape. I don't think she made it that far, this is my three-pointer. Take a look on the floor. About five meters from the vehicle there a spot of blood. I have a theory that the murderer grab the leg of the victim and she fell forward. Hitting her head onto the ground. Which caused the wound to the eyebrow she has".

"Interesting, you have a very good point professor Willincole. Dr Harpe, what weird subject are you going to say on the view you have".

"Well detective Jones for one, you starting to get on my nerve's with your nip picking. My views on the crime scene are. Similar to professor Willincole. The victim was murder here. But not restrained here. So the victim would have been tied and gagged. Making it hard for the victim to escape. This means the murderer gain the trust of the victim. Which allowed the victim to be released from the restraints. In medical terms, this would be know as sociological. Referring to, the victim who would of made the murderer believe that it was their idea to release the restraints. Two things could of happen at the point of time of the escape, first theory. The victim could of made her move when the murderer turned their back. Given the time frame it would be leased likely the victim would have made one step forward. The second theory is. The victim would of injured the murderer by causing pain. Stopping the murderer in their tracks for a split moment. The medical term, by hitting pressure points within the body would of cause a reaction. Making the person sub-paralysis. Where the person would roll around in pain. Unable to do anything. Calculating the time frame. The victim would more likely made the meter's in distant before the murderer grabbed the leg of the victim. Causing the victim to make contact with the floor. This is my theory on taking everything into account".

"Yes, both of you have very good points, thank you for that Dr Harpe. Sorry for my comments I try and keep them to myself in future".

After finishing with the crime scene. Detective Jones went back to the station with the professor Willincole and Dr Harpe. Collecting the reports of the officers and letting them go home to rest for a few hours. Before detective Jones shut the investigation room door and headed home his self. Parking up outside his house. Detective Jones switched off the engine and locked the vehicle. Has he walks toward the front door. Detective Jones notices the parcel on the doorstep. The exacted parcel, a white shoe box with the red ribbon tied neatly around the box into a bow. This time, detective Jones didn't bother to open the box straight away. He knew exactly what was in the box. So he left it on the side by the front door. ready to pick up and take with him later.

Chapter Fifteen

CHIEF INSPECTOR'S OFFICES

Detective Jones open his eye lids. Glimpsed at the clock on the bed side cabinet and whispered to his self. "Five forty-eight, Jesus man is that the time". Sitting up he sends a text to Sophia. Informing he will be at her for around ten tonite.

The Bedroom was square with tatty carpet that had cigarette burns in it. With wood chipped wallpaper. A wardrobe and chest of draws perched together. With a double bed and a large window that had a net with dirt on it. From never being washed.

Detective Jones quickly freshening up and headed for the kitchen. He pours himself a coffee and sat down at the table. Flicking through the reports from the officers. Packing them back away.

It was a fair size Kitchen with black marble top. Cooker, fridge freezer and sink with a plate rack. The cupboard was brown and black set of toaster, kettle and containers for biscuits, tea, coffee and sugar. The table was placed in the centre of the open space with four table chairs. The wall where cream and the floor had a stone effect tiles.

Detective Jones grabs the shoe box on the way out. Putting the shoe box with the reports into the boot of the vehicle. As detective Jones enters the investigation room. There was a complete silent. Placing the report and shoe box down. Detective Jones pulls the ribbon of the shoe box and removes the lip. Taking out the letter carefully. Then hand the shoe box to detective 'O' Brien for her to take it to Sophia. Has he read out the letter to everyone within the investigation room Listened.

"Right boys and girls. I need you all to listen very carefully. What I am about to read is another letter from the murderer. So it top priority we all get this right!.

Dear Chris,

Yet again you screwed up. Another victims life gone. All because you made the wrong moves. Check mate you lose again. This one got to me, broke my heart. Yes, I have one. She made me trust her. Like every other woman out there promise you the world. So like an idiot. I gave her an inch, the bitch took the fucking mile and that piss me off. Just like my so call mother. Gave me promise after promise and nothing to show for it. That why I let her rot out in the cold churchyard. For everyone to see. One thing I notice the priest took it well. On this bitter morning. Anyway, after I got over the pissed off mood. I actually felt butterfly. When watching her life fade away. Last thing just got rid of that hat. The bald patch is not that bad. If you that skint to get something better. I lend you a loan or even buy you one as a present. I do believe it time for the clues you been waiting for, here we go.

As the light turns to dark. A tinned house sits upon a holiday park. Only one floor with an eight birth. A young woman says bye to her friends who leave her and head for the club. While she gets ready before hooking up with them later on. As she gets out of the shower and enters the bedroom with a double bed. A hand grabs her from behind. She struggles, then nite nite. laid on the bed. Waiting for the time to come. The eyelids will open, a fear will come. Maybe a chat might calm her, maybe not. The pain will hurt. After that, she will drift away. Giving me the things I want. As I leave her to be found by her friends.

There you go, I leave eight clues for you to work on. Two days you have and no more. The clock is ticking. Will you make

it this time, or will it be another checkmate. You decide. So till next time, will chat again.

Yours sincerely
The Scalp Slayer

I need all of you to study this letter. We need results, guys. I'm going to be a while seeing the chief inspector Karl So the time I get back I want to hear you come up with something that going to nail that son of a bitches ass. That all for now, get to work".

Detective Jones left the investigative room. Picking up the paperwork from his office. As he walked into the Secretary's office. Heather indicated to go straight in. While detective Jones stood there waiting in front of the chief inspector's desk. Ear wigging on the conversation the chief inspector was having on the phone.

"Yes, madam chief commissioner, I understand. You must understand we under pressure here. My staff are working around the clock. I will make this case my priority. Yes, the next time we speak there will be results. I know you not happy. Thank you madam chief commissioner. Speak to you soon".

Placing the receiver down the chief inspector Karl begins to speak.

"What the hell just happen!. That was the madam chief commissioner on the phone. She not happy, with the case. So explain to me. How the fuck you and your team has come up with jack shit and why that fucking murderer is still running about murdering victims. Not sitting in one of these cells ready for questioning".

"Well, Sir it was like this. Me and my team are trying to put the clue together and to come upon the location of the areas where the murderer will hit next".

"Not good enough!. Don't want to hear that you putting clue together. I want fucking result!. I want to hear that you know the location of the murderer. I want to know that the next victim is safe. Not fucking taken away in a fucking body bag. Are my staff a bunch of idiots who can't seem to pull their fucking fingers out of their assholes. What a bunch of wankers you all are. You know what I should be doing. Handing out P45 and telling you and your staff to not let the fucking door bang all of you on the ass, on the way out".

"Sir I have results, it…"

"It what?, I don't want to hear I have results. I want to see them!. In black and white. Do you understand me!. Otherwise, there will be head rolling and your will be the first".

"Yes sir, I am sorry sir".

"I don't want to hear your sorry. If I have to speak to the madam chief commissioner or deal with her shit again!. Because you and your team haven't got results. I rip your head off and shick it where the sun don't shine and do know where that be?".

"No sir".

"Up your asshole!. So get out of my sight and get me result. One more thing. I told you detective 'O' Brien was to work with you as a partner. So why are you both working separate? I want to see you and detective 'O' Brien working together do you understand me".

"Yes, Sir".

Handing over the paperwork to the Chief inspector Karl. Detective Jones left the office and headed back to the investigation room. He enters the room and walked up to the desk by the evident Board. Grabbing the desk with his hand. Detective Jones flipped the desk over to it side making any contact that rested on the desk fly across the room. With the loud bang. Everyone in the room jumped. While detective Jones paste around the room a few time before speaking to the staff.

"I know you all looking at me wondering why I did that. I tell why. I had to listen to that complete asshole of a boss who just ripped the shit out of me. Do you know why? Because you lot can't put your heads together and work as a team. Which means I not happy and when I not happy you lot will pay for it. So if you don't want me nagging you. Start given me results. Because if I have to see the chief inspector Karl for another bollocking I will have heads rolling, trust me. Now, enough given you lot a bollocking. Down to business. So what do we have? Professior Willincole what your spill on the situation".

"Well, detective Jones. I have taken a couple of things into account. The first thing I like to get across is I was reading an article about the case we dealing with in the new paper. I read it out:

The Scape Slayer investigation by Julia Rosco,
    Another victim body was found today in the chapel of rest graveyard. The body was found by father Joe this morning. When we spoke to father Joe. Father Joe said he was shocked by what he had seen. Never in his forty years of service has father Joe come across such an all deal. He sends his sympathy out to her family and will be holding a special Sunday service for the young victim. He went on to say that father Joe had to cancel the funeral that was book for today. When I spoke to the detective in charge of the case, detective Jones. he said we are working around the clock to catch the murderer before the next attack. At this present time, we have evidence that my team are looking into. But no leads at the moment. This as been a great concern to the people in Grimsby and Cleethorpes. That is putting everyone on edge. This is Julia Rosco reporting and will keep you updated on anything that comes in regarding the story of the murderer Scalp Slayer.

Now I just thought of an ideas that might make the murder come out of hiding. My proposal is if we say to the reporter that we have someone in questioning for the murderer of the victims and believe that we have the right person. Leaving a crime number. For any information on the case. Could make the murderer angry and bring them to maybe call us. where we can trace the call and locate the murderer hideout. Getting back to the clues. I overlook the letter. The eight clue are one. Time, It get dark around six thirty, sevenish. Second. A tin house, eight birth. I believe that is a caravan. That sleeps up to eight people. Three, it will be on a holiday park. I believe there to big holiday parks and one or two small caravan home site in this recent. Four, a young girl staying with her friend in this caravan. Five, the young girl does this in a routine by letting her friend leave.

While she gets ready before meeting them. Six, the murderer is more likely be hiding in the caravan waiting for the time to strike their victim. Seven, the murderer will murder the victim in the bedroom with a double bed and last of all, eight. They will attack after the victims showered. Putting all this together I have a theory that the caravan will be located on one of the larger parks. It will be in an area where most holiday-makers will be at the club. Given the murderer, time to do what they need to do and less chance of been seen. One more thing the murderer will enter the caravan during the time the young woman is in the shower".

"I Take that into consideration what you said professor Willincole. Also, I will speak to the reporter regarding the white lie. Only because you have a very good point. That will roll the ball in your favour. Dr Harpe is there anything you would like to add. That could help with the case".

"I would like to put my views across on the evident's that we have. My view is, reading over the letter I pick up on a number of things. That gives me a greater deal on how the murderer behaviour comes across on little things they written within the letter. The murderer thives over the point of knowing that we never prevented the murder of the victim. Like the person confidant's in getting away with it is growing. Medical terms, a person who gets away with the crime build up confident and will learn from mistakes by getting better at what they do. This has made the murderer boost about it. Picking out are mistakes. By pinpointing that we screwed up. By letting the victim get murderer. Rubbing it in our faces that we lost and been checkmate. Given the murderer the pleasure of winning a game that they are playing. Knowing full well. The clues only give part of the case and that chunks which could be the vital clue in stopping the murderer in their track are missing. Like I said early the woman was using sociological abilities to gain the trust of the murderer. That sent rage throughout the body of the murderer. Medical terms, when the person gets angry. The heart rate and testosterone, will increase the cortisol know as stress hormones. This will decrease the left hemisphere in the brain. Making the person more likely to do something they would not usually do. A normal person would feel regret and guilty. In this case, the murderer is more likely use this to their advantage. Not even bat an eyelids with no regret or guilt. The murderer seems to get an sexual emotion when the victim life ends. maybe the murderer is necrophilia. In medical terms, necrophilia is a person who has sex with the dead. Also it a person who gets a sexual attraction toward the dead. This is what the person is feeling. At the time, the victims they murder passes away. There a point when the same thing happened with their mother. Where the person in their childhood place trusts in the mother. The trust was more likely broken between the murderer and their mother, not just once. It would have properly been a number of times through the murderer childhood. That would have determined the trust between the mother and child over time. The last thing is the bond between the murderer and you detective Jones is growing stronger. As they haven't taken your bald patch as a joke. This time, they offered you a loan or even offered to buy a hat as a present. Which means they haven't got an issue with the bald patch, it the hat you have".

"You pick up on some very good points there Dr Harpe, an interesting one as well. I just like to say. As a friend just to speak a bit slower as it very difficult to take everything you say. Kelly do you have anything you would like to add like a vision".

"Yes, I was touching the evidence, to get a feeling. The vision I am receiving is. A caravan with two doors. one door has just steps to walk up. The other got a step with a wooden footpath that goes around the side of the caravan and stops at the door, It lounge is a light brown with kitchen. With a door that leads to other rooms. As you go through the door just to the left is a shower room. Next to that you have to toilet. On the right is the first bedroom. Opposite the shower room. This is the room with the double bed. There a young girl. She opens the shower door. A towel wrapped around her walking into the room with the double bed. There a black shadow. No, no! she hasn't seen it. It's it g-got her. A sharp pain in the left arm. I think she made contact with the door when struggling. The room is spinning, blurred and a darkness. That all I can pick up on, nothing else".

"Thank you, Kelly, one last thing before I wrap this case up for today is the victim name is Rebecca Robinson, Mid-twenties and is married with two children. I need two officers to go around. Speak to the husband. Still waiting for forensic to send any evidence they find in the victim's vehicle. Otherwise, I see everyone in the morning".

at that point, detective closed up the investigation room and headed to Sophia.

Chapter Sixteen

THE WHITE LIE

Morning arrives, the sunshine beamed through the curtains. Detective Jones wakes, turns over and hugs Sophia, kissing her on the left cheek.

The room had pink walls with wallpaper dado rail going around the centre of the wall. With the window that had curtains on either side of the window. That were reddish pink and a style black metal pole to hold them up. The wardrobe was two wardrobes either side of each other with a mirror and dressing table in the centre. The floor had a thick fluffy beige carpet with a thick fluffy white mat. Double bed with silk sheets, pillow cover and a thick duvet clover with pink flowers in it. Two handcraft bedside cabinets and a pink lampshade hanging on the light.

"Morning beautiful, want a drink".

"Yes, love, tea with two sugar".

He gets out of bed, dressing his self before going down to make the drinks. On the way, detective Jones peeks into the bedrooms of the two children. As they sleep and closes the door quietly not to wake them up. Sitting down at the table Sophia comes down. Putting her arms around detective Jones neck and kissing his neck gently before she ran her hand across the back of his shoulders. Sitting opposite him. As she gazes into his eyes. Detective Jones swallows his last drop of coffee, placing the cup into the sink.

The dining room was a large room with light blueish wall and wooden pine flooring. There was a glass cabinet resting against the wall. That had plates standing up sideways on the shelf and cups hanging on little hooks.They all were designed with a Chinese picture on them. Just underneath the cabinet glass doors was a cupboard with two doors. The table was against the window with six table chair and two of them was in between the window and table. The window Just had a net curtain hook up on a rubber pole. With a big fish tank, that was resting against on of the walls.

He holds out his hand to Sophia, grabbing her hand. They walked to the front door. Kissing and holding each other for that few second before their bodies parted. Where detective Jones heads to work. With Sophia standing as she watches detective Jones drive off into the sunlight. When detective Jones arrived in the investigation room an echo of silence filled the empty room. Till the room started to fill up with others. An hour or so passes by. Detective Jones walks over to the evident board and faces everyone in the room. He looks around watching his staff working, some typing and some speaking on the phones that had been fitted last week. With the free call crime number. As the last caller had finished. Detective Jones started his morning speech.

"Morning everyone. Just a few minutes of your time. Today I'll be speaking to the press about the white lie. To draw attention of the murderer. In half an hour the phone line are going to be fitted with a recorder and a tracking device. If anyone receives or think it is the murderer on the other line. Place your arm in the air. Placing your thumb and index finger, to perform a circle. Doing this will alert us that the murderer is on the line. Which professor Willincole has had years of experience in this field of work. He will start the recording as we all listen on the microphones. During this time professor Willincole will be tracing the caller. So it priority the officer who is taken the call. Unless the murderer demands to speak to a certain person. That we keep this person online for at lease four minutes. If not, everything we have prepared for. Will be a waste of time. Which we don't have time to waste".

As detective Jones finish what he was saying. Officer Allen the brother who was called Jake. Of one of the twin brothers spoke out.

"Sir, just have one thing to mention, I spoke to Mrs Elison Smith a few minutes ago. She was saying that. She has an idea who the murderer is and where they are. This could be a good lead sir".

"It could be, it can also be another crank caller. You and your brother go and see Mrs Elison Smith, take a statement. I like you and your brother to look into this. If you do come up with any leads. Contact us and do not approach the murderer till we arrive. That all for now, everyone back to work".

The day passed through quickly. A spot of lunch and then detective Jones went off to the meeting with the press. To announce they had a subject. They are questioning in regards to the murders and believe that it was the right person. The time passes by while they sat quietly waiting for the article to be released in the evening newspaper. An hour before it hit the news on the channels hoping the murderer would read or listen to the white lie. Dr Harpe walks in holding the evening newspaper. Ready to hand over to detective Jones.

"No, Dr Harpe. I give you the pleasure to read this one".

"Thank you, well here it go's:

The investigation on the Scalp Slayer murders by Julia Rosco,

Today detective Jones announce they had arrested a Mr chin-lin for the Scalp Slayer murders. Detective Jones was also attended by the chief inspector Karl, detective 'O'Brien and the two M.I.5 agents. Dr Harpe and professor Willincole. Who Just stood next to detective Jones. Not saying a word to the press today. Detective Jones also mention Mr chin-lin has been charged for the three victims that were brutally murdered. Kayleigh Southan was the first one. Found in the alleyway of Freeman Street Market. Donna Mroczkowska became the second victim. murder in her house while the two small children had been drug with chemical substance and the last victim Rebecca Robinson. Was murder and found by father Joe at the chapel of rest in the graveyard. Detective Jones said Mr chin-lin was arrested at five this morning. When they receive an amnonouse call. Given the evidence of Mr chin-lin whereabout and proof Mr Chin-lin, connection with the three murder women. Detective Jones went on to say. Items were seized from Mr Chin-lin house. That contain evidence of all three murder victims. Mr Chin-lin denied this at first. After a number of hours of questioning Mr chin-lin admitted to everything. Saying he was still playing the game. Detective Jones said he was happy with today adverts that had given him the results. He and his staff had worked around the clock to bring the murderer in. Detective Jones said that madam chief commissioner Mandi Wright is pleased that Grimsby and Cleethorpes street are safe once again. Knowing Mr chin-lin is in custody and won't be murdering any more young woman. Detective Jones doesn't know when the hearing will take place. By reassuring that justice will reveal itself and Mr Chin-lin looks to be going away for a very long time. I will be bringing you more update on this story and following the outcome over the next few weeks. Up to the date, Mr Chin-lin is sentenced.

I believe that this is going to be the one. That will make the murderer angry and causing the murderer to make a mistake. In medical terms, when a person is angry they will make a rational decision. This is where people make mistake. Causing them to leave evidence that leads us to arrest the person."

"Thank's for that Dr Harpe. One thing professor Willincole were did you get a name like that, may I ask?".

"Well, detective Jones. The name came from a man I arrested in the nineties. Mr chin-lin was a serial killer. That boiled his victims in a saucepan to remove the flesh and skin from the bones. Till this day, none of the bones have been found. Mr Chin-lin would cut the victims body into parts. Placing them into the saucepan of boiling water. Eating the flesh that had been boiled and the skin that separated from the flesh. He would make furniture from the skin. It was quite a strange story. I was young and new to the job. Been at M.I.5 only a couple of weeks. Just came out of university two weeks prior. After passing my master degree in criminal minds. It was the start of the summer. The heat was unbearable. A lead came in. So I went to see this woman. She was complaining about the smell coming from her neighbour's house. Saying late at night the sound of an electric saw and rotten meat smell, linger in the air for weeks. I Stop by, spoke to the lady. Even had a cup of tea with her. Drinking out of the fineness china cup. I member her well, lovely old lady. Told me some stories of the old days, during her life. I was young and eager so I took it upon myself to investigate the house next door. Walking up to the door I pull out my handgun. knock on the door and shouted. M.I.5 agent opens the door or I break it down. The door open slowly. I remember the smell still to this day. As the door widens. I felt like throwing up. A short man head appeared around the door. Mr Chin-lin I had complains about the smells coming from your place, from neighbours. Can I entre and have a look around. I need to check thing out. Mr Chin-lin open the door to let me in. I walk into the hallway. Following Mr Chin-lin, through the house and into the kitchen. He offers me a cold drink, usual I pass. This time, I just said a glass of water would be fine. He took a bottle from the fridge contain water and poured it into a long shaped glass. While drinking the water I felt funny, dizzy and the room started to spin. I couldn't remember blacking out. When I came around I was tired to a wooden chair. In a room that was cold, damp and had a very frosty smell to it. At that time, I really through it was all over for me. But has time progressed. I somehow managed to free my arms, from the tape. I sat there making out that my arm was still tired. The man comes in. He didn't say anything. Just used his tongue like he was sucking something up. Into his month ready to swallow it. Licking his lips at the same time like he was enjoying a meal. He turns his back to me, sharping his tools. The sound went right through me. They were that rusty it made a squeaking sound like scraping your nails down a chalk board. That feeling when a shiver run down your spine. Causing you to squint your eyes. This gave me a chance, I pulled out the pen knife that I use to open letter with. Cutting through the silver tape. I manage to free myself. Jumped up, lifting the wooden chair I was sat on. Smacking it across the man head. Causing the chair to break. The man fell forward, turning around. He put his hands around my neck. Tightening the grip, making me gasp for air and we struggle for sometime. I managed to take him down using the defence classes technique, I took. Handcuffing him to a gas pipe that was running along the floor. I was in the basement of the house. I looked around other rooms to see what evidence I could find, before calling it in. There was nothing. I was about to give up looking. Till I saw the bit of string hanging out of the ceiling on top floor. I dragged the hallway cabinet. Placing it just underneath and I stood onto the cabinet pulled the string toward me. As I open it, a ladder came down. I decided to investigate. Came across a room in the attic. Noticing the furniture was different. Looking closer at the furniture. The lamp shade, couch and the back of the mat were made from human skin. The hair from humans was used to cover the top part of the mat to give it a carpet effect".

"What an amazing story, that one for the books. Now we wait to see what happen. Fingers cross everyone."

They all sat in the investigation room, clock watching. Waiting and waiting. For that one phone call. A couple of hours had passed. Detective Jones began to give up on the hope the murderer would even ring. He was ready to call it a day. Turning around, to faces the staff. Detective Jones got ready. To tell them to finish up and go home. Before he could say one word. A phone rang. An officer answers the call. With a voice recorder, that changed the voice of the person who was speaking on the other end.

"I wish to talk to detective Jones, no else. Just him".

The officer places their arm up and reveals the signal. To inform the murderer was on the other end.

"Detective Jones the person wishes to talk with you".

Taking the receiver of the officer. Detective Jones connects the device at the back of the receiver on the listen part. While professor Willincole starts tracking the caller. Everyone else stood quiet and listened to the conversation.

"Hello, who am I speaking to".

"You know exactly who I am. Think you have the Scalp Slayer murderer in your cells. Ha, ha don't make me laugh. I not going to let my artwork be taken by some kind of unknown person who is beneath me. They shit on my shoe. I am the frames Scalp Slayer. Everyone will honour me, respect me and salute me. How dare you stand their detective Jones. Announcing lies to the press. Think I am an idiot, far from it. I am always ahead of you detective and will always be ahead".

"I understand that, tell me. Has this upset you in anyway".

"Upset me, Nooo. Not upset me. Made me angry towards you. Let me tell you something detective Jones. Do you know why I pick you and it not because you're in charge. I picked you for one reason. I needed a person to target. Not anyone, someone who crossed my path sometime in my life. A person I wanted to become friend with, looked up to and respected. But nooo. You took it apon yourself. To break that chance of a friendship that could of blossomed. For years I had your picture hanging in my comfort zone. Stabbing it with anything I could get my hand on".

"Ok, why don't we start again. Maybe there a chance we can build on this friendship".

"tooo late!. You had your chance. Scewed it up like everything else you touch in your life. Don't think I haven't reliased everyone listening to are conversation. I not an idiot. I know you are recording and tracking this call. That why I have a blocker. A little device that prevents intruders hacking into the location of this call. Do you understand detective Jones. your not going to track me down. So I can speak as long as I like. You just can do jack shit about it".

Detective Jones hints to the professor Willincole to swich the tracker off. Keeping the conversation recording.

"Yes, I understand. So why don't we have chat. Now you decided to call me".

"Oooh, we will detective. I haved plenty to say on my part. Your I don't know. Put it this way. I was angry. Not the fact you lied. The fact you rip another piece out of me by cheating!. Yes, cheating in the game we are playing. Not playing it fair. By trying to check mate me without take the king. I don't like cheating bastard. They the scum on this earth. Now we may of cross path earlyer in are lifes that didn't work. Which I despise and hate you for that. That doesn't give you the right to change the rules to are game. Rules are there for a reason. So this is how it go's. I give you a clue and you have to try and stop me. Not to lie, by tryig to make me mad so that I will make mistakes. That not going to happen. I am to careful when I play my game. I check everything, double check everything. I plan, check, check again and make sure everything is watertight before I strick and make my next move".

"I see, so you like to play a tough game. Don't you think we are going to stop you in your tracks. By stopping you murdering anymore women. It might not be today, tomorrow, next week or even next month. I will get you, that one promise I keep".

"We see what happens, detective Jones. If you think you're big enough, bring it on. It sooo going to be fun knowing I am getting to you. Eaten away inside you, little by little. Face it, your getting too old for this job. Take an early retirement. There just no fight in you anymore. You know what, your just a sad old man. Trying to salvaged anything you can. By trying to bring anyone down to your level. Not me, I going up in the world. The world is my oyster, the apple of my heart. Something you will never be a part of. You had your chance and screw it up like everything else. I must say it been such a pleasure talking to you. Instead of are little love notes. We must do this again, sometime in the future. You might strike it lucky. Giving us a chance to chat, face to face. You never know, bye, bye. Detective Jones. Till next time.

"I Just want to know one thing. At lease give me that. When did we cross paths again".

"I give you a riddle and let you work it out. Then I must go. Very busy, got plenty to do before the big night ahhh!. Get what I mean detective Jones. Here we go, are you ready. A time come in our lifes, we play, we work and then we rest. As we run around, we hide and we seek. some will skip and some will kick and every so often we bat. A time will come to add or minus. Even in some case the play becomes the work. So let the work do the spelling and maybe a chance to be the best. After the day is out we rest in a way to suit. maybe watch t.v or maybe sleeping. What every makes it best".

The phone go dead, on the other line. detective Jones places the receiver down. Knowing it was not the time to stop the murderer in their tracks. There always be another day.

Chapter Seventeen

THE CARAVAN SITE

The night became bitter, with a greyish and reddish sky. While holidaymakers leave for the entertainment within the clue. A young girl hugs her friends. Leaving her along to get ready to meet them later on in the night. Locking the door to the caravan. She knocks back the alcoholic drink. Undressing herself, wrapping the beach towel around her body. She walks into the small box shower room. Hanging the towel that was around her onto the hook on the door. As she showers herself. A hooded person walks up to the door of the caravan. Carrying a toolbox. Using two hair clips. The hooded person, inserts them into the keyhole. Twisting them a few times. Till a sound of a click, come from the keyhole. The hooded person, turns the lock and pulls the handle slowly to prevent noise. Which might alert the young woman. Leaving the toolbox in the lounge, out of sight. The person creeps to the door that enters into the hallway. Opening the door. Giving them full view of the shower door and bedroom door. Waiting around the corner not to be seen. standing there, listen to the young woman trying to sing as she shower. Clutching a rag in their hand. The music coming from the shower room switches off. A click of the lock on the shower door. Before it swing open. The young woman enters the bedroom, switching the light on. The hooded person quickly flies around the corner. Grabbing the young woman.

Placing the rag over her face. There a struggle for a few minutes. Till the young woman flops, falling to the ground.

The woman is average in height, skinny body with long dark brown straight hair. her crystal brown eyes had average eyelashes. Button nose, with rosy lips and an oval shaped head. The towel wrapped over her smallish breasts. Reaching down to the top of her knees. She only had a thin ankle gold chain on her right leg. With her toes and fingernails varnish in a pattern style. her arms and legs were skinny. With the rib cage showing slightly and the every bone in the back spine appearing in her skin.

While the person listens to the music on the disc. They brought with them. Sitting there, watching and waiting for the moment the young woman opens her eyes. At this point the person had already tied and gagged the young woman. Laying her on her back. She laid on top of the double bed, resting her head on the pillow. Waking up, she felt like she had been on the razz all night. Her head was spinning to the dozen. A feeling of sickness with pin and needles overtakes her body. The person releases the woman has taken a bad side effect to the chemical. Giving them minutes or maybe seconds before the victim slips into a comer and passes away. They pull out a small glass brown bottle from the toolbox. That has a plastic ring in the top of the bottle. With a small hole in the middle. Just big enough to fit a needle in. Pulling a syringe out of one of the containers in the toolbox. filling it up to nought point seven five. They quickly hold her arm out, feeling for a vein with their index finger. By injecting the needle into the vein they releasing the solution in her blood stream. The sweat dripped down the person's face while they waited. With the solution in the woman body. It begins to work. By wiping out any chemical substance that the woman was getting a bad side affected from. Her body slowly made a full recovery. Just in time by preventing the woman from dying. The person wiped their forehead. Knowing it was a close one and it was the first ever victims to take a bad reaction the chemical substance they were using. She begins to awaken still drowsy. Knowing there was something wrong. As she had not clicked on yet. To being tired and gagged. Everything was fuzzy to her. She didn't know time, date, where she was or if it was a dream she was stuck in. This feeling went on for several minutes. Before releasing the situation. looking up at the ceiling. Terrified of her surrounding. A person appears in front of her view, removing the object from her mouth.

"Don't scream or I will cut your tongue out. I just want you to listen. I not going to hurt you. nooo. I don't do that kind of thing, That to me is sick to overpower a woman, take advantage and hurting her. Them kind of people. They the scum on this earth. I like to talk to my victims. Explain exactly what I will be doing. There will be pain, lots of pain. As I remove the organ from your body. While keeping you alive. Once this is done, you can drift away. Move your head if you understand!. Good to know. Now let me tell you the story. It's all about detective Jones. You'll properly wondering who the hell is that. It the person who is in charge of the investigation. You see my name is the Scalp Slayer. There you go, your eyes just answered the question. So I take it you heard of me, how exciting!. It sends goosebumps all over my body. Someone who know me by my name. I alway said to myself, I'd be frames one day. There you go it only take one person in this world to know my name. So if you think one person knows my name. With my name being broadcast in papers and televisions across the world. That one person becomes millions, making my more frames than anyone in the world. Don't you think so?. I know and your eyes never lie. Where was I. Yes, detective Jone? We had a chat me and him. Do you know why. He lied to the press. About some man called Mr chin-lin. Saying He was the Scalp Slayer. Mr chin-lin, I know who he was. A person who separated body part and boiled them till there was no meat left on the bone. Eating the flesh and making furniture from the skin and hair of his victims. A certain person arrested Mr Chin-lin in the nineties. Professor Willincole, he one of the guys on detective Jones team. Master of criminal Minds. I let you in on a secret. Professor Willincole will never be able to understand my mind. Do you want to know why? Because it too late for me. I come too far and there no turning back. My brain had it. I just got no humility left in me anymore. After professor Willicole, arrested Mr chin-lin. He didn't even make a year in jail. The guards let him out when everyone was locked in their cell. They call that numbers in there. So if you're a sex offender, grass or murder children that were you go. Till one day a prisoner was let out by the guards. Turning a blind eye. Mr chin-lin was beaten so badly. Not even the morgue recognise his corpes after the prisioner had finished with Mr Chin-lin. Getting back to our story. Detective Jones has it in his head. He's going to take me down. I couldn't stop laughing, my side are still hurting. Now there something between me and detective Jones. I am going to tell what that is. I know him a long time ago. Believe it or not we started pre-school together my mother who I don't like to meantion because she nothing to me anymore. Was best mates with his mother. So over the year I respected, looked upto him and trusted detective Jones. I Kind of had strong feeling toward detective Jones, until this one day. We started senior school together. Like every other school we went to. I was being bullyed by other kids. At that time I found it hard to protect myself. Detective Jones turned away when I beg him for his help. Do you know what that does to person. It eat away inside you till there nothing left. Till one day something clicks in the brain. That exactly what happen to me. Detective Jones will pay in time. There a serect, he has a daughter. To an ex-partner. I'm just waiting until the daughter is the right age. Then detective Jones will pay for everything. I going to take her life. Leaving detective Jones with no family relation in his life. It will kill him. He love her to bits. He would even walk to the moon and back for her and I am going to take her away from him. So now you know what I have suffered over these years. I believe she turn a teenager. So that means five years to go before the big event. On her eighteen birthday, I even film it. So detective Jones get front row seats. Watching his daughter life being taken away. Shhh I see light beamng throught the close cutain, let me take a look".

The murderer places one hand over the woman mouth Using the other to peak out of window. Then went back to what the murderer was doing. Before they where interrupt by the lights.

"This so excites me, I am here with you. They about thirty minutes away, give and take. Checking every caravan. I can see their lights in the distances. The game as up itself. It could go ever way. Not for you, the time as come. Any last word or sins you like to get off your chest. Say it now or hold you peace".

"Please I am too young, let me go I beg you please".

"Pity won't get you anywhere. Your sins will be forgiven".

Piercing the skin. While holding the hand over the woman mouth. So it would dim the sound of her scream. The tears rolled down the side of her face. Has her eye glazed over upon her lifeless body. The murderer slips away. A few more second would have brought it to an end. The officers blow the whistle, to attract attention. Detective Jones enters the caravan. Feeling the body for a pulse. Walking back outside. His team standing around the caravan waiting for his answer.

"She dead, body is still warm. Only thing this time. Her inside are still hanging out. This means the murdered didn't get the time to complete everything. They only manage to cut a little under half the scalp off. This means they had to rush, not given them time. If only we were a few seconds early. We could have prevented the young woman in there, losing her life".

Turning round looking into the dark night Detective Jones shout out at the top of his voice.

"Next time, we will have you Scalp Slayer. I keep to my promise. We are getting close and closer. Every day you be looking over your should. Till that day comes when I'll slap on them cuff's and bring you in. I know you are listening to what I am saying. I have all the time in the world. Detective 'O' Brien call it in. Go to reception and find out the names of guests staying in this caravan. I want all you officers to seal off the area. About fifty-yard perimeter. Professor Willincole and Dr Harpe have a look round and see if you can come up with anything".

Detective 'O' Brien calls it in over the radio. Before heading off to reception. While the officers run the police tape. Around the area to seal it off. Detective Jones sparks a cigarette up. Taken a few big drags before stamping it out with his foot. Looking around, into the dark areas. Whispering to himself.

"I know you watching. Somewhere out there. I can feel your presents. Keep watching because I going to wipe that smile off your face".

Just passed the tape the murderer sits looking over at detective Jones. Just enough distance not to be seen by anyone. Still given a full view on everything. Listen to detective Jones. The murderer smiles. Also whispering to themselves.

"Let the games begin. The fun as started. You still lose detective Jones. That what you are a loser. It time to go. I leave the shoe box here. So you know how far I was from you. Even mention it in the letter. Bye for now, till next time".

Disappearing into the night. Back to the safe zone. the murderer goes. An hour later Sophia turns up, in her van. Pulling out the equipment she needed.

"I just hear, you nearly had the murderer. That this victim inside, been left in a total mess, love".

"Yes babe, I had the murderer in the palm of my hand. Only if I'd made it slightly earlier. The murderer would of been locked up by now".

"Don't worry about love. Don't let it get to you. There always next time. You are a good detective. Who always get the job done. Just look at last year. You got a medal for the detective who hasn't lost one case, yet".

"I know that babe. I hold a hundred percent in solving cases. I like to keep it that way. This one not going to get the better of me".

"And you will love, I best get on now. Come to mind tonight. I cook your favour meal".

"I will babe, need the company".

Sophia went into the caravan. While detective Jones was still looking into the dark areas.

"Heather, come here".

"Yes, sir".

"I want you to walk over there. Go pass the tape a few extra meters and take a look into them bushes. I don't want you to walk straight over. I want you to walk around. Follow the holiday park around to the other end and backtrack. Till you come in from behind the bushes. One thing before you get close. You going to need to be extra quite treading. We don't want to alert anything that could be hidding in there, do you understand me".

"Yes Sir, you want me to creep up on the thing hiding in that bush over there".

"You got it in one, report back to me".

"Ok, sir"

Officer heather heads of to the outer rim of the holiday park. Before backtracking inwards. Toward the bush that was inches away from the tape. Detective 'O' Brien comes back from reception.

"Detective Jones manage to get hold of the guests staying at this caravan. I informed them about the situation. They getting hold of her family to let them know. Also got information on the victim. Her name is Lauren Bruce, she in her early twenties and still live at home with her parents. Not far from here. She lives in Grimsby. They book the caravan for a fun weekend. She not into sitting around watching shows in the club and she waits till the disco starts. Before she comes out to meet up with her friend".

"Thanks for that detective 'O' Brien".

Sophia came out to update detective Jones.

"Love, it the same person. You can tell. Every cut, position and angle match the other three murders. They just didn't have time to finish up".

"Thanks babe, I going to leave you to finish up in there and head back to the station".

"Ok love, see you later".

Sophia went back into the caravan. While detective Jones headed toward officer Heather. As they meet up She hands him the shoe box with a red ribbon tied around it.

"Where did you find it".

"Just in the bushes, you said to look in. There no one there sir. It was just sat underneath the bushes".

"Ok thanks".

Detective Jones walk of the crimes scene. Heading back to the station with the shoe box. To take time to think. Before the rest of the team got back.

Chapter Eighteen

A CLOSE CALL

The next morning had arrived. Detective Jones sat holding his coffee. Stiring it with a teaspoon. Whiles thinking about the next move on the case. For once in his life. He had never come across a case like this one. No criminal had outsmarted him. The way the murderer had done. Detective Jones was on the edge of throwing in the towel, given up. Maybe the murderer was right. He was properly getting too old for this kind of work. But then there was this little spark that went off within his head. That kept his ego going. Detective Jones stood up. Placing the coffee down. Saying to himself. No, I will not let this person beat me in any way or any form. I going to see this though, all the way. This time, you be the one down mate. I will stop you in your tracks. Everyone sat there listening to detective Jones. Wonder if he had lost the plot. Detective Jones didn't relased he was saying it out loud. Instead of saying it in his head. He turns around facing his team, they say nothing to him. Knowing full well they heard every word he said. But just keeping that moment to themselves.

"Morning boys and girls. These pass few days as been a rollercoaster for us all. We work overtime, around the clock. Everyday as been a new challenge for us. Where we come that close to revealing the murderer. Then there was the last hurdle that we can't seem to get across. Putting us back at square one. So what are we doing wrong, nothing!. We are doing everything right. But not looking at the big picture. So I been thinking all last night. Right up to now about this and came up with this idea. We needed to start looking at the big picture. From different angles. Not what's in front of our faces, what are faces can't see. By doing this, we need to think about what in the box and also what out of the box. Then putting them together. To reveal the answers we need to solve this case. As the answer is smacking me in the face, but I am ignoring it. When I should be using it, to our advantage. Are you all following me on this?. If not and you not understanding I'll put it in layman's terms. We got to start thinking outside the box. This is where we are going wrong. So till we start doing this. The murderer is going to be running around freely and we ain't going to stop the murderer in their track. I am going to read the murderer letter which was found in the bushes at the holiday park yesterday.

> *Dear Chris,*
>
> *What a game we had yesterday. It was a close call. You came so close to stopping me, never mind. You can't win them all, maybe next time losers!. I was there, right in the bushes. Watching you all in full view. You could have out smarted me. Sending your team around the back way. Trapping me in. But nooo you stood there mouthing off. So I left the box exactly where I was, so you would of know. I must say this, you screw up my artwork. I wasn't finished with her. Didn't even get time to have sexual impulse. From watching her eyes. As she passed away. Like I did with every other victim's. That had crossed my path. Not to worry. Plenty of time for that. Let me tell you something. Ever heard of a person called Rosemary, think back. She was my first, begged me and told me, she loved me. The hate inside me, never had pity on her. I just stabbed her that many times. She was unrecognizable. Left her body to rot in the cellar, of a house. Mothers ahh! who needs them. Clicked have you!. Yes, it's Rachel. The one that grew up with*

you from a toddlers age. Who fell in love with you and you just throw it all back in my face. That day when I was being bullied, I cry out for you and you just left me. We could have had something special. Now don't think you got me. Because you know who I am. A few years back when you was not around. I was trapped in a house fire. Ended up with ninety percent burns. They didn't think I would pull through. They were totally wrong. After all the plastic surgery's, my looks changed. So the pictures you have in your head of me. Are not the same. I look totally different. Interesting ahh!. So when I found out where you was after taken care of my mother and a few more victims on the way. I decided to study you. I being in your life for ten years now. You never know, I been watching you all this time. Planning my revenge, on you alone. I murder more victims than you know about, Just never left them out to be found. Except these ones, for some reason. Come on Chris think about it. The game we playing. For me to involve you I have to leave a victim laying about so an investigation could happen. Nobody, no game. So now you kind of know who you looking for. Make it more interesting. Let's play.

I walking my pet, through a load of trees. A field is near by. Containing a play area, where you can purchases food or drink. The main road nearby. Fitted a light, so my pet could be seen. As when it dark in there. It hard to see. Who could be hidden from me? While grabbing me, the pet nowhere to be seen. I waken to find, I am restrained. A chat to come, before the pain. It time to go. Towards the light. Where I will entre, the spirt world.

There you go, you have the clues. Two days, no more. The clock will tick, hands will move. will you save or will lose. It up to you, if you like to win. let see, what you achieve.

Your sincerely
The Scalp Slayer."

After reading the letter out for the first time detective Jones sat down. He couldn't believe what he had just read. It had been years and the memory's he had were gone. Just the name was the one thing he remembers of her. Not one day had passed. Till this very day did he ever thing about her. Now it was time to take her down. So detective Jones could move on with life. So he built up the dutch covrage and stood up to take charge of the investigation.

"I don't know what to say. I am speechless. But I am going to say this. That was then and this is now. I knew her back then when we were kids, I don't know now. That just make her like another stranger. That I will be putting her away for a long time. It was just the shock of the old roots appearing again. It time to remove these old roots. Let's take this bitch out for good. So guys start thinking outside of the box. So by tomorrow, we have the Scalp Slayer in are cells. I have you two hours to go over the evidence. Then I am getting feedback from you, that all for now".

Detective Jones walks out of the investigation room. Head for a bar in town. To have a couple of stiff drinks. Making sure he had some strong mints to take the smell of alcohol off his breath. Finishing the drinks, detective Jones looked at the clock behind the bar. Time was getting on. Popping a mint into his mouth. Detective Jones headed back to the station. Walking into the investigation room. As he heads towards the evidence board. Turns and faces the staff. Detective Jones begins to speak.

"Afternoon everyone, I like all of you to pay attention. Early on today I read a letter. That has revealed the murderer real first name. Her full name is Rachel Harrington. Now we have the name, we need to find the whereabout of Racheal. This is what going to happen. I want all officers in this room. To get out there, checking every building in Grimsby and Cleethorpes. Going through Council offices, banks, state agency and hotels. She has to be staying some where. Paying some kind of bill or even getting money. She can't be far and there no way any person can live on thin air. Still managing to pay for equipment and items she is using. No one in this room is to release the information we got from this letter. To the press or newspaper. Do we have an understanding?. I don't want her to escape. I want her caught so I can she the bitch burn in hell. Professor Willincole is there anything you would like to add".

"Yes, I been going through all evidence so far. Putting bits together to get a general idea of the kind of person this Rachel is. My theory is, she as a lot of mix motion over you detective Jones. Hate, love and jealousy. Because of this, she has becomes your stalker. Causing her to change the way she murders her victims. To put it across, before she never revealed her victims. Till now, were she is leaving the victims out. For you to find and to play a game. The reason is she loving the fact you are given her all the attention. That you never gave to her when you were children. There a part in the letter were she said. "She been in your life for ten years and you never know". This could mean two things, she follows everywhere you go. Which she could be sitting outside the station waiting to follow you. To where ever you go next. The other thing is she could be someone in your life now. That you know like, friend, lover or someone at work. Didn't it say "she had ninety percent burns and had plastic surgery". So how would you really know detective Jones? It could be any of these women in this building. As it sounds like Rachel as had a total face lifted. There will be one question I like to know. What her mother did to her to make Rachel take her mother's life in that brutal way. Reason is something happen there. Rachel never went into detail on this subject. Like she did with you, on the way you treated her. The riddle, I believe that it a park with a wood in it. Rachel going to murder the victim in the woods. When the victim is walking the pet, that is a dog. This victim must take the dog for a walk in the evens. The reason I think is the dog. Doesn't get on with other dogs so the victim finds it better to walk the dog at night when no one is about. So the clues, well I already gave you the place, the pet, wherein the place and time of day the murder will happen. So we are halfway through the clues. Item the dog is carrying, glow sticks. You shake them and they glow, plastic glow stick that can be bent around into a circle and the victim will use it like a collier for the dog. Rachel is going to wait till she let the dog of the chain. Properly drug the dog by given it some meat with a drug that been injected into the meat. Before attack the victim. The day it happens, alway's two days. That's one thing Rachel does. Murder and then misses a day. Why to study the next victim before

Rachel go in for the kill. Last of all, time it takes to murder the victim. The last victim, we interrupted Rachel. She wasn't happy that Rachel didn't get the time to finish up. On all the others Rachel tucked the insides of her victim back into their bodies. Alway's took the top of the victim's hair off. The last victim was different. Her insides were still hanging out and only half was taken from the top of the victims hair. So I think Rachel must of seen us coming when we were walking through the caravan site with touches. While checking every caravan. Given Rachel time to disappear before we got to the victim. That all I am going to say for now".

"You have a very good point on this. Thank you, professor Willicole. Dr Harpe what medical view are you going to give us today".

"The best medical advice in the would, detective Jones. Sorry, I had to say that. It was what you just said. You see, Rachel is suffering from a mental health condition. Self-esteem, lack of confidence. Not in looks, intelligence or confidence to talk to people. It more like racheal had her emotion taken from her. Causing her emotion to go all over the place. In one case I dealt with:

It was Christmas week and we just may a big arrest. Member the big story on the winter murders. For years, victims were being murdered during winter. Then it would stop and start again on the next winter. This went on year after year until the big day when we caught the murderer. I still remember to this day, Mr Thomas Jeck. His emotions were all over the place. One minutes he was laughing, then crying and when the anger came the whole world could hear him. Mr Thomas was a very confusing guy. By saying one thing, then coming out with another thing. Mr Thomas would say, I murdered her laughing and Joking about it. Two seconds later, he'd be crying saying, I didn't mean to, I wasn't there and it wasn't me. Then suddenly angry would come. The fucking person pissed me off. I fucking glad I ripped their fucking smelly shitty inside out, the wankers had it coming to them. I basically put it down to split-personality. When I ask him why only winter. He came out with this. Why not winter, you have mid-summer muders. Which I knew it was a program as it one of my favours. Then Mr Thomas, went on to say. The bodies don't smell as bad after leaving them

for a couple of day. Before cutting up the body and then getting rid of the body parts. In the cold wintes, It was always my favour part of the year.

You see Rachel kindly reminds me of Mr Thomas. She hates you in way that she wants revenge. But love you too as she doesn't want to murder you detective Jones. In medical term emotion play a big part of everyone life. There are so many different parts of emotion. to go through them. I properly be here till tomorrow so to break it down you have love, hate, jealousy, angry and happiness. They are just a few of them. This is a first, changing tack-tits. Rachel always got rid of the victims to make sure they would never be found again. Only leaving her mother. I think Rachel mother was a trophy. She may of hated her. But the one piece in her heart was the memories. By keeping her mother body where Rachel could find her. It will alway keep the memories of the mother. So when we do arrest Rachel. We going to find the mother close by. Rachel put in the letter "mother was in the cellar". Assuming the person she stabbed was the mother. Then started to leave the victims in the open for us to find, to play a game. Professor Willincole you were right on that. Rachel was looking for attention. In medical terms, when a person is not showing their attention. The other person starts to wonder why. So they will automatically change, by doing something they never did before. Now if the person not showing attention. Begins to show attention. The person believes this way as work, so they keep on doing it that way. Rachel used the victim as bait to draw your attention detective Jones. The games, it was always about the clues Rachel gave. The last thing I like to say is when Rachel had plastic surgory. She might have learn from that how to remove body parts back then".

"Very good points their Dr harpe, liked the story too. Kelly what vision have you got for me today".

"Well, detective I had a shocking vision. It's was about you. I saw you walking down some stair. I believe a cellar. There a dirty sink on one side, with a mirror that missing the left top corner. That broken off. On the other side is a fridge freezer. On the other side of the room. against the wall is a body. It female, I can tell by her clothes. She looks like she been their long time, as she started to rot. The walls are white and the floor is just stone. The other one in the letter. Just can't seem to get a vision".

"Ok thank kelly, don't worry about the other vision. You help us with this case a lot. I'm grateful for all your help. Well, guys tomorrow is the big day. It the day Rachel goes after her next victim. It also the day we are going to stop Rachel and celebrate a job well done. That what I want to see tomorrow. Everyone get off, see you all in the morning and don't forget to start the search. I want a lease three hours of all you officer searching flat, houses and business before you clock off and go home tonite that all thank you.

Chapter Nineteen

TRUE IDENTITY

The next day had come, a mobile rings on the bedside cabinet. Detective Jones reaches over, picks up the mobile and answer the call.

"Sir, you not going to believe this we think we have the Scalp Slayer in the cell. You know you sent us on them house search yesterday. Well, this woman started to run. We manage to stop her. When we ask her name she wouldn't tell us. Found a letter with a name Rachel on it, in her house. She not talking".

"Right, I'll be there as quick as I can. Keep her in the cell till I get there. Then I take it from there".

"Ok, sir".

Detective Jones quickly get's dressed. Go downstairs. He makes himself a coffee, sits down at the table. Reading the yesterday newspaper, while drinking the coffee. As he finishes off the coffee. Detective Jones grabs his coat on the back of the chair. A coin falls to the floor and rolls. Resting against a cabinet. Detective Jones walks over and bents down to pick the coin of the floor. Noticing just through the gap at the back of the cabinet was a door. It puzzles him a bit as detective Jones never know there was a door Because of the cabinet being there. He pulls the cabinet to the side without disturbing the plates and cups in the cabinet. Revealing the door in full view. Standing there for a few second wondering to go through or not. Detective Jones ego in wondering what was on the other side got the better of him. He turns the handle, opens the door. A very bad fusty smell come from inside. Detective Jones, didn't think nothing of it. The stairs went down, into a pitch of dark. So detective Jones switch the light switch on the wall at the side of him. Lighting the room up that reveals it was a cellar. He walks down the stair till he reaches the bottom. It was just like the same kelly had said yesterday. Sink to the right with a mirror, missing a piece at the top left corner. Fridge freezer to the left. White walls and stoned floor. At the far end of the room was a body in female clothes. Rotten that the skin had turn greyish. There was no eyes just maggots eating the inside. With flies buzzing around the body. A cardboard box was sitting underneath the sink. Detective Jones go over to investigate what was in the box. Flipping the lid open. He comes across a book contain pictures and hair inside the book. Noticing the victims he had dealt with were in the book too. Aslo, there was picture with other picture. like a family album. He put everything back and closed the lid. Next to the box was a toolbox with different department. Detective Jones decides to open it up to see what was inside the toolbox. Two knivies with blood stains, ropes, rags, two chemicals substances in brown glass bottle, box of plastic Gloves and a roll of aprons. Closing the toolbox and standing there. Detective Jones heart was beating to a dozen. Detective Jones reaches inside the coat pocket, pulling out his handgun. Check to see if he had bullets still left in it. Making a call on his mobile phone. Detetive 'O' Brien pick up the receive.

"Detective 'O' Brien, how can help".

"Detective 'O' Brien, it detective Jones. I just want you to listen and then end the call. Forget that person in the cell she not the Scalp Slayer. I come across something. Evidence of the Scalp Slayer murder's. I need you to go and have armed police ready. Track my mobile phone it will give you the location. Trust me".

At that point detective Jones ended the call. Detective 'O' Brien rush down to the investigation room and flew through the door.

"Guys, just had the call from detective Jones. He only found evidence on the Scalp Slayer. Told me to get armed police and track his mobile phone for the location".

Professor Willicole runs a chase on detective Jones mobile phone. Coming up with the location he quickly writes it down on the back of his hand. Gearing up before leaving. Everyone got into the vehicles. Seven police cars, three police vans and an undercover police vehicle. With siren going. Flashing blue light. One by one went out the police gate. Heading to the area where detective Jones was. Following each other in a straight line, on the roads towards the location. Detective Jones held the handgun. Pointing it outwards as he went upstairs. She stood there given detective Jones an ice-cold look. Making her move by pointing the handgun at her. She sits down at the table, detective Jones sits opposite her and begin to speak.

"I'm confused. Just can't believe what I am seeing. Explain something to me. I know you as Sophia Portess or do I now call you Rachel Harrington".

"Call me what you like, got a new identity. It wasn't the genral identity I never legalley change my name. only my surname".

"And the kids, do they know".

"No, they were too young at the time. They alway believe my name to be mum and even believe my first name to be Sophia. They no nothing about this at all".

"Why!!!."

"You really want to know why. Come on detective Jones, think about it. I hate your guts. But the love is still there. As much as I hate you. I couldn't see you dead because of this little part of me called love, it stand in the way. So I start from the beginning, shaw we!. After surgery was done. I notice I was not that person I looked like. Before the fire and surgery. When you was out the picture. I had a breakdown, it was hard. Mother never was around. Her drinking problem made it hard. Cleaning her sick up, having to put her bed. Everyday she promised that she wouldn't have another drop of drink. but nooo! she carried on. To one day I picked up that Knife. Stabbing her, couldn't stop. Just carried on. Before her last breath she said

173

"please don't, I love you pleeaasee" that was it not another word out of her. I must of lease carried on for another five minutes putting that knife into her lifeless body. It felt good, it felt sooooo gooood!. So I started murdering victims, had a busy life then. Went to school and became a Doctor. Working with the dead. Now you got amit that is a perfect job for me. As I get the best of both worlds working with dead and making my victims part of the dead same things ah!. Even met my husband at working. Now I had feelings for him. But the feelings for you were much stronger. I married him in ninety-four. Became Rachel Portess. A year later gave birth to the twins. A boy and a girl. I think I stop murdering around that time. Motherhood just doesn't give you anytime at all. Six months passed and a fire in the house. I grabbed the boys first wrapped it in a dripping wet blanket running through the house. The whole downstairs was lit up in flames. I could feel the burns and the pain as my flesh was being burned by the naked flames. I carry on, the boy was out. Then did the same with the girl. I was burned all over. Heading back to help my husband. There was an explosion. It blow me off the ground. Hitting the floor thirty meters from the house. The next thing I know. I woke up in hospital on machines. The doctor came spoke to me. said "Mrs Portess, your kids are safe. They being looked after by a caring family till you get better. Bad new is your husband die in the fire. He's been buried by his family a little over two months ago. I know this is hard for you. There nothing you could have done. You have been in a coma for three months. During that time I'll given you plastic surgery. Because of the injuries, I had to restuctor your whole face. So when we take the bandages off you won't recognize yourself". Mother was safe, at the time she was still in the cellar of her own empty house. Till I move her to this house when I decide to find you. Stuck her in the boot of the car, she been frozen that long it took hours for her to defrost. Still to this day I never sold or rented that house out. It's been left empty for now. A year passed got out of hospital picked up the kids. started murdering againt. This is where I got the tease for a womans womb. It was by pure accident. I went back to work. A young woman's body came in. About in her early thirties, unspected death. Was running late that day. Had to be home for the babysitter. It was to do with the womb, I think it might have been cancer. We'll never know. So I took it home with me. Stuck it in the food fridge for me to test later. Ooops never got that far. Wasn't looking, pulled it out of the fridge. Cut it up and cooked it. I had the best meal, I ever eaten. I wanted more of that same meat. Only thing is the meat I wanted was the womb of a woman. Which I supposed of tested. Didn't release till I was ready to test the woman womb. So gave the death report a load of cobbler. Said the woman died of nature causes. Then from that day, I started cutting out the womb of my victims. Why do you think I was offering you to come back to my place every time we met at a crime scene of one of them victims, ahh!. I tell you why. Your favour meal you enjoyed eaten. Do you know what was in it? the wombs of the victims".

Detective Jones face turn whitish. His mouth watered and a sickly feeling came. Horrified by the fact he had eaten a woman womb. It just wasn't right. All he wanted to do was grab her and smack the hell out of her skull. but he was not going to bring his self to her level. Racheal carried on talking.

"Anyway enough said about that, we carry on!. I decide it was time for payback. So I came looking. Tracked you down. Notice you was just getting promoted to detective. So I applied for the job at the police station. Then we met. Became friend, still hated you then and still hate you now that will never change. So I waited a bit longer to have my revenge on you. Still had that love that alway got in the way. We became friends with benefits. know as fuck buddies. Always studying you every day. Then you went off to London. Didn't see you for a bit. we talking six month. Still was caring on with my victims. All the time I been up here. You never suspected a thing. Then I was having a spot of lunch to eat. Hear one of the officers talking about you coming back from London. This was it, I planned everything whiles you were away. You know cross the t, put the dots that kind of thing. There it was when we were kids. My dad, when he was alive you remember Him. He was the best chess player. Taught me how to play. So I took the style of play. Which was always think eight step ahead. Gave me the idea of the clues to give you. Then there was the name. When I was little. I picked a book up. It was a story about cowboys and Indians. There was a part in it where it said about the Indians cut the hair off, so the spirit can't be pulled into heaven. Gave me the perfect name. The Scalp Slayer. Now I couldn't give you my real name. It would take all the fun of it. So I decide that these victim will have the tops of hair slice off. Even greater, your like this one. Got about thirty, maybe more empty shoe boxes. In the cuboard under the stair. Had to get rid of some of them shoe boxes. So I bought some red ribbon and decide I use them to send your evidence present in. Good ahhh! and last of all the victims. I had to leave the bodies to start the game. You just played it like a fool. That why the Scalp Slayer knew everything about the case and where to leave the shoe boxes. Studying the victims were easy. You had the ones that did the same thing every time and the one that didn't. That were social media come in. Everyone puts details of what they are getting up to or doing that week on social media. The problem is, they never lock the public out. So how do you think I knew about the victim at the caravan. Social media people will never learn and that a fact. I could of carried on and on. But you too nosey and had to go spoil everything didn't you detective Jones. Well done you won your first chess game. Let me go and print you a certificate".

As detective spoke. He was still trying to prevent himself from being sick.

"You are right about one thing. I am a fool. To ever have met you in my life. This is the time I wish I could of turned the clock back. I wouldn't of brought you back to my mum, when crying in the park. Because you was lost and my mum wouldn't of taken you home. While waiting to find your mother. Then are mothers wouldn't of come friends".

"Now detective Jones. Are we spitting are dummy out again. Come on you was a toddler like me. Even if you turn the clock back. There still ninety-nine point nine percent the same would happen again".

"How many victims have there been".

"Couldn't tell you off the top of my head. Give you a rough figure. Hundred or more".

The sounds of siren. Flashing light filled the streets. Blocking each end of the street with a prisoner carrier parked outside house. As the front and back door got busted in. police from both sides rushed into the room where detective Jones and Rachel sat. Detective Jones started to read her rights.

"Rachel Portess, I am arresting you for all the murders you have told me today. Anything you say will be used as evidence in the court of law. You are in title to a lawyer, if you can't afford one you be given the choice of having the state prove you one. Do you understand your right?"

"Yes".

Putting on the handcuff's he got detective 'O' Brien to place her into the police van. before she disappeared. Rachel said one last thing

"Just one more thing I like to say. If you think prison is going to hold me. You have another thing coming. I will escape. Five years from now the big event is coming and I got the best seats in the house for you detective Jones. This one going to end you. When it does, I completed my revenge on you. Bye detective Jones".

Detective Jones sat gazing out of the window. Watching detective 'O'Brien place Rachel into the back. Locking the cage gate. Closing the double doors. As Rachel was drove off to the station. Soon as the van disappeared out of detective Jones sight. He rushes off to the bathroom throwing up knowing he had eaten human and not even know.

THE END

**A special thank you to all the people
who wanted to be in the book:**

Kayleigh Southan
Jessica 'O' Brien
Kelly Ramsden
Donna Mroczkowska
Rebecca Robinson
Mandi Wright
Lauren Bruce

Lightning Source UK Ltd.
Milton Keynes UK
UKOW04f0017250817
307915UK00002B/67/P